SINS AND INNOCENTS

Burhan Sönmez

Translated by Ümit Hussein

SINS AND INNOCENTS

Published by
Garnet Publishing Limited
8 Southern Court
South Street
Reading
RG1 4QS
UK

www.garnetpublishing.co.uk
www.twitter.com/Garnetpub
www.facebook.com/Garnetpub
blog.garnetpublishing.co.uk

First Edition

ISBN: 9781859643846

British Library Cataloguing-in-Publication Data
A catalogue record for this book is available from the British Library

Typeset by Samantha Barden
Jacket design by Andrew Corbett
Cover images Collage by Andrew Corbett.
Photograph of tiles © Tanuki Photography, courtesy of istock

Printed and bound in Lebanon by International Press:
interpress@int-press.com

For Kewê

CONTENTS

1
FERMAN

A Lost Star

My motherland was my childhood; as I grew up I became distanced from it; the more distant I became the bigger it grew inside me. In those days Uncle Hatip, who hoarded all the secrets of Haymana Plain like a poor dervish, would drop in on us on spring mornings before the household was awake. Before switching on his radio he would fill my mother in on the latest news of murders, women who had left their husbands to run off with their lovers and newly orphaned children. Life for him was a road that crossed sunken bridges. He would take his tobacco case out of his shoulder bag crammed with pistols, prayer beads and lighters and, standing at my bedside, roll himself a cigarette. His fingers were cracked like soil. As he drank his tea from a patterned glass I would think about the sounds that collected in his radio. I wondered whether he had brought me the end of last summer's half-finished story that I was afraid of forgetting. I suddenly remembered he would only be staying a week, before setting off for distant destinations once again. My heart would swell with a melancholy that would haunt me into adulthood, and which I believed I had inherited from my mother.

I coveted the happiness flowing from my uncle's slender hand as he stroked my hair.

My mother would sing Ferman's folk-songs to my uncle. If you included all the dead, there were a lot of people in our small village. My uncle would listen to the songs and reminisce about the old days.

Years before I was born Ferman had given his heart to a timid girl called Asya. The moment he returned from his military service he dispatched the village elders to request her hand in marriage. The girl's brothers opposed the match with head-spinning vehemence and hurled insults at the elders acting as intermediaries. Upon receiving the bad news Ferman recalled the sea he had seen during his military service. He realized that the dread of obliteration, common to all steppe-dwellers and that had assailed him when his ship had remained at sea for three consecutive days, was about to become a reality here in his own village, and he resolved to abduct Asya. But the next day his cow failed to return from pasture. They found its corpse by the stream. The following night twenty lambs disappeared from the pen and the pile of straw on the threshing floor went up in flames. When, one morning, he discovered his dog's body riddled with knife wounds and its amputated tail tossed onto the roof, he knew his turn would be next.

An enduring grudge, of the type that adolescent boys relish, had led Asya's two brothers to keep Ferman at arm's length after some petty squabble they could barely remember. This harmless hostility may have gone on forever had that rogue not set his sights on their sister, escalating bitterness into bloodlust and threats. That knife called honour concealed in every heart was ever ready to spill blood. Asya, who for years had built her hopes on dreams of Ferman, was now as desperate as a child who has fallen into a well, weeping as she listened to cries from the outside world.

It was the end of winter and the ground was covered with snow. Ferman now slept during the day and hid amongst the rocks in front of his house at night, ready for the next attack.

The night he saw that one of the two youths approaching from the direction of Asya's house was carrying a gun, he was convinced they were coming to spill his blood. He pointed his rifle and shot the tall one first, then the other one. My father knew a ballad about a similar tale. In the song he used to sing, trying to emulate the beautiful voices of the village epic tellers, a young boy quarrels with the family of the girl he loves and kills six of her brothers, leaving only one alive to continue their line, then lives happily ever after with the girl, who is called Kejê. "Kejê Mirzobege, gul sore, por drêje," my father sang.

Strange though it seems to me now, having reached the age I'm at after living in densely populated cities, studying in large schools and travelling in foreign countries, in those days I never tired of listening to this ballad in which men didn't think twice about killing the brothers of the girl they loved. Each time I listened to it I would fall asleep, locked in the embrace of tradition, as content as if I had reached the stars. But Ferman did not sleep, not that night, nor any other night thereafter. He ran with everyone else who had got up at the sound of the gunshots and saw that the two people lying on the ground were his own brothers. According to eyewitnesses he lost his mind on the spot and, howling like a dog, vanished into the darkness.

Ferman's two younger brothers had gone to Haymana to study. Ferman had no other family and, proud to be the brother of the first boys in the village to go to school, had started to dream of their future. He hadn't been expecting them to suddenly appear before him one night. On the first day of the school holidays the two brothers had travelled halfway in a horse and cart, spent one night in the house of the cart owner and set out the next day with a gun he had lent them to protect them against the hungry wolves. They had walked all day, and were on the verge of collapsing with cold when they met their deaths at the hand of their brother.

No one ever mentioned the brothers' names, neither Asya's rancorous brothers nor Ferman's brothers, who had died before they could read all those unknown books. They loomed over evening conversations like nameless gravestones, incapable of making everyone accept that they were the real protagonists of the tale.

For years Ferman lived in caves, valleys, at the base of rocks. Afraid to sleep in the dark, he would scream in pain greater than that of the wounded soldiers he had seen in his childhood, singing mournful songs. Asya's velvet-toned poet encountered coffins during the night; he was not only separated from his beloved, but his brothers' blood was also on his hands. A destiny we all fear more than death hung around his neck like an indelible inscription. In one of his laments he sang, "I don't know where the sun comes from/Or where it now sets."

Mecnun meant someone possessed, and was used to describe the love-crazed, those who had been cast to life's furthest bank. If Leyla's Mecnun had been possessed by love, lost his mind and finished up in the desert, then Ferman was twice *mecnun*, having fallen victim to the demons of both love and death. He became acquainted with every hollow, mountain and deserted spot on the plain, wandering in the darkness and only succumbing to sleep at dawn when the tight knot in his heart gave ever so slightly. Gazing at the stars he would pray for his pain to ease. Ferman had never been a saint, and entertained no such notions when he lost his mind and took to the plains. He was simply possessed by love and death, living with his own demons and awaiting death in his own darkness. As the poet said:

> *Just because you toil and slave night and day,*
> *Do you fancy yourself life's creator?*
> *Listen to the tales of all whom time has turned to dust,*
> *Destiny rules all hearts,*
> *It opens every door and slams it shut at whim.*

One summer's day, while crossing the east side of Mangal Mountain, Tatar the photographer came upon Ferman asleep behind a rock and, recognizing him not from his appearance, but, like everyone else in the region, from his destiny, stood there in the blazing heat for a while without moving. Then, concluding he had nothing to fear, he took his camera out of his bag.

When Ferman awoke from one of his anguished dreams to the sound of the photographer's shutter, the two men were as startled as two lost Turkish and Greek soldiers coming face to face during the war that had raged on that mountain twenty-five years earlier. They stood taking deep breaths under the rising sun as though they had journeyed thus far together. When their eyes met, each knew the other would not harm him. Tatar told him he had spent the past two years on the plain wandering from village to village, taking cut-price photographs, and was now on his way to deliver the photographs he had taken the previous summer. Ferman uttered the name "Asya".

Tatar the photographer arrived in the village in the afternoon and, ignoring the curious gazes of the girls and young brides by the fountain, headed for Kewê's house. My grandmother Kewê and her last husband Haco were sitting under the apple tree. Tatar mentioned Ferman, who had stared at the photos, transfixed. Ferman, who had seen that the people he knew had changed and aged, believed a mirror would appear under each photograph and show him his own face, which he no longer remembered. When he had lived in his village his world had been a simple one, circling its timeless orbit day after day. But now he was lost, shooting from one place to another like a star that didn't know where to rest.

"When he saw Asya's picture he sat as still as if he too had tumbled into the black and white photos," said Tatar. "Then he left all the other photographs on the ground, stood up and walked off into the distance, leaving his gun and saddlebag behind. When I told him I was going he didn't answer or notice that I had left the bread, cheese and tobacco in my bag beside his saddlebag. It was only then that I saw the black horses behind the rocks."

The photographs Ferman was holding in his emaciated hand and studying at leisure were as distant and as frightening as that winter night sixteen years ago when he had shot his brothers. Before he knew that the past would haunt him forever, he had hoped to escape from its horror by running away. He believed that place conquered time and that time conquered pain. They buried his two brothers without him and locked up his house. As if in atonement, Asya's parents died within one month of each other, the old wounds they had attempted to push to the back of their memory throughout their lifetimes still fresh in mind. Those were times during which it was a virtue to ransom your children's sins. Asya, now prone to fainting fits, no longer spoke to her brothers, who, for their part, had abandoned her. Instead of living in trepidation of Ferman returning to wreak vengeance at any moment, they chose to depart to a land about which little was known except its great distance, and soon their names were deleted from the common memory. Although their early lives were governed by where they were born and bred, they later joined the ranks of those who denied that was the case.

When my mother, aged ten on the day Tatar the photographer arrived, told these stories years later, she referred to everyone, good or bad, as "innocent". Particularly when talking about Ferman, Kewê and the Claw-faced woman.

When the Claw-faced woman arrived at Kewê's house to ask if she had seen her daughters who had been missing all day, everyone knew she was afraid of photographs. However, trying not to let it show that she was afraid of the photographer too, she took the purslane she had picked from her garden out of a corner of her dress and put it in a bowl. She looked at Kewê and said, "My girls are nowhere to be seen, Asya hasn't seen them either. I thought they might be with you." Although the Claw-faced woman's two daughters were now adolescent, they ran around the village all day, giggling and behaving in the flighty manner that everyone was now used to instead of sitting demurely at home and awaiting their destiny. Of all the elderly people in the village Kewê was the one they respected most.

My mother, who was a quiet, introverted child, said, "I didn't see them paddling in the stream today."

"Ah Kewê, if only my daughters were as sensible as this girl of yours," lamented the Claw-faced woman. Kewê reminded her that it wasn't the first time the girls had been late home and told her not to worry.

Once the girls had sat until the early hours with a ewe who had lambed the previous month. Then they had chased after the horse and cart of a pedlar because he hadn't been impressed by any of the curses they had been hurling at him for hours. The pedlar collected clever curses, paying children for them with treats. The girls, who had been pursuing the pedlar all day, refused to return home with the villagers they met at the top of the hill, only consenting when persuaded by the Claw-faced woman and Kewê, who had got wind of the story. They complained that they had been compiling curses for weeks but that the pedlar had rejected even the really good ones like: "May the black donkey's stick beat your ma and after seventy whacks may she beg for more!" It meant going without roasted chickpeas and carob. They continued to curse at the top of their voices, swearing on the life of the father they had never met that next time they would come up with better rhymes.

The villagers had heard there was a terrible war raging some place as far away as the country where Asya's brothers had gone. Several countries had invaded each other and Germany was trying to take over the world, but they knew nothing of Stalingrad, D-Day or the fall of Berlin and thought that beyond this arid steppe the war was still going strong in 1946. When Tatar the photographer told the people who went to see him that the war had ended, no one paid much attention to him because they couldn't contemplate Germany being defeated. They were amazed to hear that Mustafa Kemal had died eight years previously and asked him why he hadn't mentioned it on his last visit the year before. "How was I to know you hadn't heard? The whole world was in an uproar, kings from all over the globe came and wept at his funeral for three days and three nights." When he went on to assert that the commander who had defeated a huge army on this very steppe all those years ago was none other than Atatürk and that he had not died of war wounds or been poisoned by foes but had expired in his bed like any other mortal, instead of believing him the villagers remembered the words of the old man Os the previous year: "Be wary of these photographers who want to play God with their fake human likenesses."

2
FERUZEH

The Western Front

"This is the only photograph I've got of my uncle. It was taken in a coffeehouse. The man next to him is Tatar the photographer. As Tatar is holding his camera someone else must have taken it."

When I finished speaking Feruzeh picked the photograph up.

Outside it was raining gently.

I had known Feruzeh for three days. On Tuesday I had gone into the antique shop in Mill Road called The Western Front. The elderly woman who owned the shop was watering her plants in the interior patio at the back. She mistook me for one of those undesirable customers who wander into antique shops to kill time rummaging amongst old objects and wander back out without ever buying anything. She carried on watering her plants, to allow me to browse at my leisure. I walked up to her.

"What beautiful weather," I said.

"Yes it is. We really needed it," she said.

"It's very sunny for April," I added.

"I'll bet it's always sunny in your country at this time of year."

She had assumed I was Mediterranean from my accent and dark skin.

She put the empty watering can on the table.

I showed her the photograph I was holding. I told her I was looking for the camera in the picture.

She took it and looked.

"Are these men still alive?"

"No," I said.

My Uncle Hatip and Tatar were sitting on stools on the pavement outside the coffeehouse. There were several empty tea glasses in front of them. You couldn't see the make of Tatar's camera; it was the size of a hand, its protruding lens folding like bellows.

"Was he a photographer?" she asked.

"Yes."

She looked first at my face, then examined the photograph more carefully.

"He doesn't look like you," she said.

"No, he doesn't," I replied.

She sat down on a chair by the table and pointed out a stool for me.

"I wish this warm weather would last a few days," she said.

She raised her head. Her drooping eyelids were ready to doze off into a sweet sleep.

"Hopefully it will," I said.

Clearly she had time for a chat.

"Do you like Britain?" she asked.

"I like Cambridge," I said.

"It's a lovely city. I was born here," she said.

"You're lucky," I said.

She smoothed her hair with her hand and contemplated the sunlit garden.

"You're right, no one grows old in the place where they were born anymore," she replied.

"That's true," I said.

She told me her name was Stella. I introduced myself.

She laughed. "I won't try to pronounce it, I'm terrible at foreign names."

The bell on the door rang and a young woman wearing a blue dress entered. I hadn't realized the door had a bell. The woman flashed me the easy smile of a hostess greeting a guest and went into the kitchen. She was carrying a carton of milk and a jar of coffee.

Stella turned back to the photograph.

"Who's the other man?" she asked.

"My uncle."

She picked her glasses up from the table and put them on.

"This camera looks like one of the first Olympus models," she said.

The woman in the blue dress brought two cups of coffee and placed them on the table. Surprised, I thanked her. I added milk and sugar to my coffee.

"I hope you manage to find the camera," I said.

Stella pointed to the glass cabinet beside the back door. It was full of old cameras.

"Those aren't as old as yours," she said. "Tonight I'll have a look at the catalogues I have at home; I might find something. May I keep the photograph?"

"Yes. I have another copy," I replied.

"Have you tried the photographer's in King's Parade?" she asked.

"Not yet."

Stella explained that after the Second World War she had worked on the local newspaper *News*. She had been interested in photography ever since.

I finished my coffee.

"See you tomorrow," I said.

I walked towards the door without stopping to admire the antique paintings, the chandeliers and wooden carvings. I saw the woman in the blue dress beside a lion statue. I thanked her again for the coffee.

"You're welcome," she replied. She had a nice accent. I don't know what she must have made of mine, but she said, "Are you Iranian?"

"No," I said.

She hesitated.

"Don't tell me where you're from, I'll try and guess."

"I'll be back tomorrow," I said. And added with a smile, "You have until then."

I went outside. The world seemed bigger on sunny days. The streets of Cambridge had grown too. I walked past language students and homeless people roaming the streets with their dogs. I gave way to cyclists. I browsed in the bookshops in the city centre.

In the evening I went to Soham for a wedding. It wasn't quite 6.30 when I arrived but from the size of the queue at the door of St Andrew's church I realized that the wedding ceremony of the African slave who had been dead for 210 years, which was going to be re-enacted this evening, was more significant than I had thought. I took my invitation out of my pocket and quickened my pace. I queued behind well-heeled men and women draped in tasteful black and red evening wear. Everyone exuded elegance I would never have witnessed had we met in the marketplace. The smell of perfume wafted all the way to the gravestones by the churchyard.

Some minutes later I noticed the woman in blue from the antique shop standing in the growing queue behind me. She was wearing a black dress now. I looked; she was alone. I joined her.

"Hello, are you Iranian?" I said.

"Yes."

We smiled.

"In the shop you seemed disappointed when I told you I wasn't."

"No, not at all," she said, almost apologetically. "I just didn't expect to be wrong."

"I'm from Turkey," I said.

"Now that surprises me. Your accent isn't at all Turkish."

Her name was Feruzeh and she worked part-time while doing her PhD in English literature.

At the door I showed my invitation for both of us; Feruzeh didn't take hers out. The church was crowded. We found seats near the back and sat down.

The speeches began. The original ceremony had taken place in 1792. A freed slave called Olaudah and a local woman called Susannah had been married in this church. It had all started when Olaudah was abducted from his village in Africa at the age of eleven. Feruzeh and I exchanged looks when we heard that.

A choir of children took the stage. They sang for Olaudah in the hold of the ship that crossed the ocean. The hold was small, damp and cramped. The slaves died either of disease or because they shook free of their chains and jumped overboard. Olaudah didn't manage to die. He became a skilled sailor and learned how to read and write. Ten years later his master set him free. He wrote a book about all the hardships he had endured and started to campaign to abolish slavery. Olaudah's book became as renowned as Robinson Crusoe. In fact both told the same story, black slaves became free by emulating their white masters. When the children finished their song Olaudah had made it safely out of the hold onto the deck and had taken a deep breath.

Once Olaudah and Susannah had been married again and blessed, Feruzeh wanted to go outside for a cigarette. We slipped away from the crowd and stood beside the gravestones. The air was cool. Feruzeh wrapped her thin shawl around her shoulders.

A young boy smoking beside us gave his jacket to the woman he was with. I tried to take my jacket off too but Feruzeh wouldn't let me.

It was too late for a bus, so we took a taxi. After dropping Feruzeh off, and giving a week's food money to the taxi driver, I came home and read poetry late into the night.

When I went back to the antique shop the following day Stella was alone.

"Hello young man," she said. "I haven't got any news for you about the camera yet. A friend of mine in the Camera Club has a huge catalogue. I'll look through that. It's bound to give us a lead."

"Thank you."

"My pleasure."

She was sitting at her table repairing the cover of an old book.

"It's sunny again today," I said.

"Thank God."

"You feel less lonely on sunny days," I said.

She looked at me.

"Are you here alone?"

"I have friends."

"That doesn't stop you feeling lonely."

I thought for a moment. I looked at the sunny garden at the back of the shop.

"Loneliness comes in all shapes and sizes, no two types of loneliness are the same," I said.

"You're right," she said. "My loneliness hits me at night."

I waited a while. Then I browsed amongst the antiques.

"Do you like reading?" she asked.

"Yes," I said.

She held up the book in her hand and showed me the battered cover: *All Quiet on the Western Front*.

"It's the first edition," she said. "Nineteen-twenty-nine."

She returned to repairing her book.

I examined the antique paintings. I touched each lampshade and wooden carving in turn. The frame of the mirror beside the lion statue was carved with rose bush motifs. I stood in front of it and straightened my glasses.

"Goodbye," I said, and left.

The sound of the bell on the door was drowned out by the cars outside. It was hot. The street had grown crowded and there was no trace of yesterday's spaciousness.

The following day I bumped into Feruzeh in the city centre for the third time. She was looking for a present for her mother's birthday on Saturday.

"This is our third meeting in three days," I said.

"Yes, people are always bumping into each other in small cities," she replied.

"It looks like you're not working today. Shall we have a coffee when you've finished your shopping?" I said.

"Yes, why not," she replied.

"I have an appointment in a few minutes. It'll take about half an hour," I said.

"Okay, I'll have finished by then. Where shall we meet?"

"You know the pub Fort St George. It's by the river."

"I'll see you there in an hour," she said.

The pub was exactly halfway between our two houses. I was late. Feruzeh was sitting in the back room at a table overlooking the river.

There was a book in front of her.

"I'm sorry, my appointment was longer than I expected. I couldn't let you know because I didn't have your number," I said.

"Don't worry, I read my book," she said.

I put the folder I was carrying on the table.

"I was interpreting for a patient at the clinic. The doctor kept us waiting," I said.

"Do you interpret every day?" she asked.

"Two or three times a week."

"Like me, I help Stella out three days a week."

"Stella's nice," I said.

"I've worked with her for a long time; she's like a mother to me," she said.

"Have you had a drink?" I asked.

"No," she said.

"What will you have?"

"Tea."

I ordered at the bar.

"Do you know, I've lived in Cambridge for years, but this is the first time I've been to this pub. I'd heard it was nice, but I never imagined it would be so peaceful," she said.

"It's always like this on weekdays. I've picked out a handful of places in the city where I like to read. This is one of them. It's never crowded. You've chosen my table; I always sit here. I watch the boats sailing past on the river. I read for hours."

I looked at the book in front of Feruzeh. It had a rose design on the cover. I guessed it was in Farsi. She turned it towards me.

"Can you read this?"

"It looks more like embroidery than writing," I said.

Our tea arrived. We both added milk. She took sugar, I didn't.

"But you take sugar in your coffee," she said.

"You're very observant."

She looked at her book.

"In the olden days everyone had a book that matched their soul. They would call it their 'book of secrets' and carry it around with them wherever they went, forever. This is mine," she said.

16

Her slender fingers rested on the book. They sat amongst the letters stretching across the page like a flock of birds.

"Does everyone in Iran walk around with a 'book of secrets'?"

"If only they did," she said.

She wore her hair in a ponytail. She had a pendant with a rose in the centre.

"Do you go back to Iran very much?" I asked.

"No," she replied.

"Is your PhD about the secrets in Iranian literature?"

"My thesis," she said, smiling modestly, "is about the influence of the First World War on English poetry."

"Why didn't you choose something to do with the connection between English and Iranian poetry? That's more in keeping with your own situation."

"And what is my situation?"

"What I mean is, as you know two languages and two cultures, you could have put them together."

"You think like my mother. I'm a woman, so I could have worked on women's issues. I'm a Muslim, so I could have studied religion. I'm Iranian, so I could have tackled the Eastern question. Why should I limit myself to those boundaries?"

"You write poetry, don't you?"

"Do you think that's a requisite for studying English poetry?"

I sipped my tea slowly.

Feruzeh went on. "Isn't it enough to write a thesis about something you love?"

"What you say makes sense. You see, I don't think like your mother."

"So you approve of my thesis then ..."

"Yes."

She drained her cup.

Then, as though remembering the question I had just asked her, she said, "My mother left Iran with me and my sister when I was seven. I haven't been back since."

"Did you leave during the Revolution?"

"Yes, when the new regime came into power."

"Do you have family there?"

"Yes."

"Your father?"

"My father was imprisoned a few days before the shah went into exile. After the mullahs came into power they said he had died. We never found out what happened to him."

"Was he involved in politics?" I asked.

"He was a university lecturer. My mother blamed both regimes for his death."

"Do you ever get nostalgic?"

"About my father?"

"I meant about Iran ..."

"I don't remember much but I do miss it, though I'm not sure exactly what it is I miss. Iran is like my father. They don't exist in the real world, they're only alive in a world that lives in my memory."

"Where would you like to die?" I asked.

"Here maybe."

"But I bet your mother would prefer Iran."

"Definitely. When I was a child and she was teaching my sister and me to write Farsi she used to insist that we would go back one day."

"A friend of mine asked people from all different countries that question as part of his research for his thesis. Most of them said they would like to die either in the place where they were born or in the place where they grew up. My friend's conclusion is that your motherland is the place where you want to die."

"Maybe. How about you?"

"I want my grave to be in the village where I was born," I said.

I poured more tea into our empty cups.

"I saw the photo you gave Stella. Is it of your family in your village?" she asked.

I opened my folder and took out my copy.

"This is the only photograph I've got of my uncle. It was taken in a coffeehouse. The man next to him is Tatar the photographer. As Tatar is holding his camera someone else must have taken it."

Feruzeh took the photo.

I told her about Tatar the photographer, my uncle and my grandmother.

Outside it was raining gently.

3
KEWÊ

The Moorland Song

When Tatar the photographer had arrived in the village the previous summer my grandmother Kewê had looked wordlessly at the camera of this man rumored to stop time while resting her back, bent under the weight of a life as heavy as gravestones, against the apple tree. Now, as she touched the photograph in her hand, she recalled her childhood, spent in a remote village. Raising her head she gazed at the tree that stood like a mute child, bathed in the shadow cast by the open door. Her ancient eyes grew dark.

In the olden days, when her father was all alone in the world with his only daughter, who prayed assiduously late into the night, Kewê had bowed her head before the sword called destiny. During her childhood, as her mother and seven elder brothers died one after the other in ambushes or from illness, she got into the habit of sitting under the apple tree in the garden day and night talking to the birds.

Death accompanied her everywhere because, many years earlier, her father had been a guest at the house of a certain *agha* and that agha, instead of serving him soup, meat stew and bulgur with lentils, had offered him nothing more than unbuttered *börek*. Kewê's father's pride had got the better of him and he had sworn a bitter oath on the life of his chestnut mare. He had no idea that the agha had been preoccupied with two Englishmen and an officer who had called on him the previous day, staying only as long as it took to drink a glass of sherbet. This agha, whose finesse had vanished along with his manners since the days when he evaded paying taxes to the Ottomans, had not slept a wink on account of these unexpected guests. Before long, the pretty girl the agha intended to marry disappeared with a man whom no one knew, and everyone on the plain – suspecting Kewê's father's involvement – knew that vengeance hung heavy between the houses like summer heat, and would soon come knocking on their door.

Kewê, who had grown up in the shadow of a curse and spent most of her time under the apple tree, was oblivious of her slender body, her snow-white complexion and her velvety voice. Which is why when Allodin, the heartthrob of every girl by the fountain, declared he loved her and no one else, she couldn't believe it. When their fathers couldn't agree over the bride price Allodin had no choice but to abduct her. Kewê was the only one who didn't know that one day, when the village girls were out collecting briar, Allodin would gallop into the field on his white horse, sweep her up onto his saddle and, adding his own cries of joy to the girls' shrieks of happiness, ride off with her towards the villages in the west. As Kewê told this story to my mother as though it were a fairy tale, she would say, "Stop Allodin, don't charge your horse towards death!" and each time my mother would think that, like all fairy tales, this story too would have a happy ending.

While pregnant with her first son, Kewê arrived on a donkey at the field where the labourers were harvesting the crops, carrying a bundle filled with lamb, bulgur and onions. When the sun had set and the crops became invisible in the darkness they all sat down together beside the piles of straw. The most spectacular stars of the plain shone down on them that night, while fireflies glowed as far as the eye could see.

The majority of the labourers were lowly souls, convinced that God had abandoned them. They had travelled from distant cities in the east bearing their scythes on their shoulders like rifles, with no other refuge than their arms, their breath and their masters' compassion.

Begohan, the labourers' foreman, had paid the price for his gambling, and who knows what disgraceful acts that he was too ashamed to repeat, by banishing himself from his home and was now purging his sins with the sweat of his brow in foreign lands, living for the day when his wife and children would accept his vows of contrition. When Begohan had finished his tale he shut his eyes and sang a folk-song. A red breeze blew gently. Forty years later Kewê sang that song, which she had memorized after a single hearing, to my mother. And forty years after that, her eyes closed, my mother sang it to me. Now, in a foreign city, surrounded by stone buildings, I hum the same song to myself at night. To enable me to withstand life, as ancient buildings do, sometimes I too close my eyes.

That night the foreman Begohan said, "Allodin Agha, if your child is a boy, name him after me." Kewê gave birth in the autumn, by which time Allodin had forgotten all about that incident and was about to find a different name when Kewê reminded him of the promise he had made beneath the stars. As a tribute to the labourers' friendship and the boundless sky, she remained true to her memory of the night when her heart beat with love and to the folk-song of the steppe.

Kewê had tied a piece of cloth around the apple tree for her dead mother and each of her seven brothers. She repeated the act after the demise of her father, closely followed by her father-in-law. But the night when her husband too collapsed on the threshold she vowed she would never again take anyone to her bosom except her four weeping children. Instead of tying a cloth around the tree, she did like everyone else in Haymana Plain who spilled blood to free themselves of the horrors of

Burhan Sönmez

blood, and sacrificed a lamb. Dipping her finger into its blood she smeared it onto the foreheads of her children, Begohan, Şemil, Sıtê and Mâna.

Life was becoming oppressive. Her mother-in-law and two sisters-in-law evicted Kewê from the farm and snatched her children from her. With the twenty sheep they gave her, her dog and her donkey, Kewê returned to the silence of her father's home. As was customary for widows, she wore her husband's jacket. She was not yet thirty when she resumed her conversations with the birds under the apple tree day and night.

One night when winter was drawing to an end her eldest son Begohan arrived, rain drenched, mud splashed and windswept, saying, "Grandma sent me, Şemil is ill." They arrived at the farm in the steppe in the middle of the night, and were at Şemil's bedside when he expired at daybreak, overcome by measles. Three days later Begohan, the boy whose name was a keepsake from a labourer with a scythe, contracted his brother's measles and followed suit. When spring passed and her mother-in-law also died, Kewê took her two daughters to live with her.

She sat her daughters under the apple tree, sang folk-songs to them and told them stories with happy endings. Her eldest daughter Sıtê was as tall and well-formed as a slender glass lampshade, it hurt to behold her. One of the childless women in the village promised Sıtê the gold around her neck if she would become her husband's second wife. Kewê opposed the match, but her daughter left to join that household. One day Sıtê, who had gone to the steppe to collect briar with the village women, suddenly fell to the ground and started vomiting blood. When they brought her back to the village she was barely moving. Kewê wept by her daughter's bedside throughout the night. At dawn, Sıtê opened her eyes and said, "Ma, you woke me from a sweet sleep." They buried her the following day and Kewê was left alone with her youngest daughter Mâna.

One morning, they were woken by the sound of drums. The Greek soldiers had traversed the whole of Anatolia, and were approaching Haymana Plain. The men were forced either to fight or to lead the life of bandits. Mothers like Kewê fled to distant villages to protect their young daughters' honour. Their only sustenance was the barley and wheat in their sack and they would stir half a handful into boiling water and drink it. They came back from behind the mountains a year later and Mâna's hand was requested in marriage to one of the young boys in the village. But on the wedding night, instead of the young bridegroom, they put his half-witted elder brother in the bridal chamber, pairing Mâna with a fool. My grandmother Kewê was convinced that she was now completely alone in the world and that she had no strength left to bear her destiny. Removing her man's jacket, she retracted the vow she had made years before when her husband had died, and married a second time.

"I came to this village and married your father because I was in despair," she said to my mother, who was still a child. "Your father Abdo was a poor shepherd. We had nothing; not a single one of my children was alive. We decided to go to foreign lands and so, loading a saucepan and a quilt onto the donkey, we set off. We roamed Polatlı, Sivrihisar, Çifteler, Eskişehir, Bozüyük and Bursa, labouring in fields, working on farms. Seven years later we returned to the village with an ox cart and a pair of oxen. With our savings we bought sixty sheep and built this one-room house."

Kewê brought seeds from the apple tree in her own village and planted them at the front of the house where she now lived, in this way reappropriating the tree she had leaned on since childhood. Sitting under the tree as she had done in the old days, she waited for the birds so she could talk to herself.

One snowy winter morning she received news of the death of her daughter Mâna. Leaving her husband sick and burning with fever, Kewê took to the road. Mâna's slow-witted husband had brought the news. By the time they reached the precipice of her native village, her feet were frozen.

Kewê thought about the Mogul girl whom the villagers talked of, who had cast herself off this precipice centuries earlier. Despair is life's most deadly executioner. A very long time ago, after the soldiers of Timur, the Mogul emperor, had defeated the Ottomans, they had stopped for a rest on this precipice and pitched their tents, which were as numerous as the stars, in the summer heat. That night Timur's adolescent daughter Mâna, unbeknownst to anyone, stole away from the camp and threw herself off the precipice. Timur, who had doted on his daughter, limped to the precipice with his lame leg. He had been injured in a battle, though he had wreaked more than adequate vengeance in all ensuing battles. Timur looked out into the darkness and the commanding stars in the sky. Shaking his fists at the sky, he shouted, "Hey Mâna!" The warriors, witnessing his sobbing for the first time, named the area Hey-mâna Plain. The name became part of the local lore and, transcending generation after generation of deaths, travelled all the way to Kewê. As the poet said:

> *Let not the new light and new hue of the dawn sun deceive thee,*
> *The fruit on the tree is green already while its name dates back*
> *to days gone by.*

It was dark when Kewê, whose last child was named for the Mogul emperor's daughter, arrived at the village with her son-in-law. A storm raged in her heart. Taking Mâna's two daughters into her arms she cried all night; towards morning, clutching them tightly, she lay down to sleep. Alone with her in the bed the two small girls said, "We're going to tell you a secret; they buried our mother alive." Kewê also heard what was being whispered in the village. When Mâna had fallen unconscious after lying in bed for three days with a high fever they assumed she was dead and washed the body and buried her. Every day the village shepherd Hilo would herd his sheep, but that day his younger brother went in his place. When the flock was passing by the graveyard, their bells clanging, Mâna shouted from under the freshly dug soil, "Hilo, Hilo, get me out of here!" Hearing his brother's name, the young shepherd took fright and ran to the dead girl's house.

The only person at home was Mâna's mother-in-law, and she said, "Don't breathe a word of this to anyone; if they take the dead body out of its grave we'll live in fear for the rest of our days."

One month later Mâna's daughters also died of measles and were buried side by side in two small graves.

Kewê, who now had no children left, decided to find a wife for her second husband Abdo and bring a new child into the house. "What are we going to do with a child, crazy woman? I'm a sixty-year-old man," said Abdo. It was 1935. Kewê asked the grandmother of a young girl called Emine who had come from a distant village to visit her relatives for her hand in marriage. She had pushed to the back of her memory the anguish she had felt when her own daughter had become the second wife of a married man.

"That day we worked on the farm," she told my ten-year-old mother. "Your father cut the crops with his scythe, your mother Emine walked behind him, putting all the stalks into a heap, and I picked up all the bits that were left behind. When Emine went into labour we came home. By morning you were born. Abdo was waiting outside. 'Crazy woman, what did you have?' he asked. 'A girl,' I said. 'Never mind,' he consoled me. Emine was dark skinned, while your complexion was white, you were a white lamb before a black sheep. The harvest ended and in midwinter your father became bedridden. We buried him one *bayram* day under a relentless downpour."

Emine was still a young girl and in the spring her elder brother Hatip came to announce that Emine had a suitor in her own village. They were sitting under the apple tree. Breathless, and with a beating heart, Kewê asked them to leave her the baby. Emine, realizing it would be better to go to her new home as a childless bride, knelt down beside Kewê and wept. And, leaving my mother behind like a tree she meant to come back often to water, she set off one day at daybreak with her brother Hatip. Life's weary ox cart plodded on. When they built a mosque in the village the old man Haco became the imam, married Kewê and moved into her house. More than one another, those two elderly souls, who had bathed in separate rivers and were both alone in the world, went to sleep with their arms around my baby mother, whose real mother lived in a distant village.

As he listened to Kewê in silence, Tatar decided to freeze time and take a photograph of Kewê, Haco and my mother all together under the apple tree. What was strange was not life but death; knowing it would never be sated it lusted after everything in its path. Haco, who went to the mosque, would return with the villagers a short while later and they would put the world to rights over tea and tobacco. There was still a long time to go before the Claw-faced woman came and shouted, "Where are my daughters?" The night was just starting and outside on the apple tree a lone bird was singing.

4
AZITA
The Sacred Apple Tree

I arrived at the main entrance of Trinity College.

I looked at the apple tree to its right. The huge door I often walked past had made me blind. I remembered this apple tree when Feruzeh mentioned it yesterday.

I walked slowly on the lawn. I touched the four perfectly proportioned branches sprouting from the trunk and circled its girth.

Two girls asked me to take their photograph. They hugged the tree. They were careful not to step on the flowers. They had come to Cambridge to study English. They were from South Korea. They asked if I knew whether the college was open for visits. As our chat continued they wanted me in their photographs too. I felt like the owner of the tree.

We learned in primary school that an apple fell on Newton's head. But not many people knew that the tree at the entrance of this college where he taught came from some seeds from the original tree in his town.

The apple tree was laden with blossom that was radiant in the April sunshine.

A young couple speaking a language I didn't recognize approached me. I took their photograph too. Just then the porter at the college entrance came and asked us politely not to step on the grass. I apologized.

The Saturday morning and sunny weather crowds were growing bigger.

I leaned against a bicycle and closed my eyes. My eyes were burning because I hadn't slept the previous night.

I didn't let it get to me anymore when I couldn't sleep. My spells of insomnia were gradually becoming shorter and more infrequent. Nowadays they only lasted a day or two. In the beginning I used to go mad with despair when nothing helped, no matter what I took, and I would lie in bed semi-conscious for days, gasping for breath, my mind blank.

Last night I had gone to bed as usual with a book. Before long my eyes started to feel heavy and I switched off the light and drifted into a dream world. My thoughts were like a stylus as it moves along a record. They started off in a wide space and were captured by the darkness of sleep when it became narrower. I was like a star spinning in the vortex of a black hole before disappearing into its centre. Nothing, not even light, could escape from the pull of that darkness. Only the sounds from outside disturbed me; the roar of diesel engines, drunks shouting. Just before midnight the large girl in the flat next door had sex, then her cries died down.

One night some two months earlier, I woke up to the sound of music and the shaking of my bedside table. My neighbour, who didn't have sex at that time of night, had invited her friends round for a party. I knocked on the door, which was opened by a woman in a miniskirt. I told them that after three days of lying awake I had finally managed to get to sleep and asked them to turn the music down. Holding a cigarette in one hand, she took my arm with the other and dragged me in. The crowd of people in the house didn't bat an eyelid when they saw me in my pyjamas and if I hadn't been so badly in need of sleep I would have accepted the invitation of the woman who said, "Why don't you join us?" My neighbour was nowhere to be seen. The woman blowing cigarette smoke into my face took pity on me and turned the music down a fraction. I went back to bed. That night my bicycle was stolen and I didn't hear the thief breaking the lock. After that day, whenever I couldn't get to sleep I would say, "They can steal my bike all they want, as long as I can sleep."

Last night's book was about a child who ran away from home to go to the stars. He smuggled himself onto a ship but it sank and he ended up on a desert island. I liked reading illustrated books at night; they sent me to sleep. But last night it hadn't worked. The stylus in my head got stuck and the disc had turned vain, interminable circles. The star outside the black hole did not get pulled into the vortex.

I opened my eyes, straightened up from the bicycle I was leaning on and crossed the road. I was tired and crouched down beside the post office.

A child pushed his brother, dropping his ice cream on the floor. His father scolded him. They went back to the ice cream van on the street corner.

A man showed me a map and pointed to the marketplace. I gestured that he had to walk towards the left.

I stood up when I saw Feruzeh.

"Have you been here long?" she asked.

"No," I said.

She looked at the impressive door of the college.

"This door reminds me of giant wall rugs," she said.

"Excuse me, are you Iranian? Is there any chance that you might be Iranian?"

"Yes," she said, laughing.

"When I look at it from a distance I see the same thing," I said. "But when I get closer the patterns of the rug disappear and the oppressive shadow of aristocracy looms."

We walked towards the apple tree. Feruzeh noticed my happy expression.

"You look as though you've just met up with a long lost relative."

"Is it that obvious?"

"Yes."

We didn't go up to the tree. The college porter was standing in front of the door.

"I took some photos for some tourists while I was waiting for you. If you've brought your camera I'll take your picture too," I said to Feruzeh.

"I didn't bring it. But it's you I should take a picture of."

"Next time," I said.

"Is this tree anything like the one your step-grandmother grew?" she asked.

"Ours was bigger."

"Yours …" she stressed.

I nodded.

"I read that this tree comes from the original one that grew the apple that fell on Newton's head, but it hadn't occurred to me that it had the same fate as my grandmother's tree, taken from its original land," I said.

"They planted this tree here long after Newton's death."

"Don't tell me it's only a legend!" I said.

"To banish all doubts about the tree's origins there was an investigation and it was proven that the two trees were related."

I smiled. "That's typical of the English."

No one asked us to take their photograph. They always approach people who are by themselves.

I pointed at the door of the college and said, "Shall we go in and look around?"

"I haven't had breakfast," said Feruzeh.

"Where would you like to eat?"

She thought for a moment. "I'll choose the pub today."

"Okay."

Leaving the apple tree and the huge door behind we started walking down the street.

On the street a girl was playing Vivaldi's *Spring* on her violin.

We strolled past buildings that tourists were admiring with rapt attention. We walked past Great St Mary's Church, which gives a spectacular view of the whole city from the top and where the theologian Erasmus preached five centuries earlier, past the house where Fitzgerald, the first person to translate Omar Khayyam's poems from Persian into English, lived two centuries ago, past King's Chapel, the stained glass windows of which were removed during the Second World War so they wouldn't be damaged, and veered left.

The garden of The Eagle pub was full, so we sat inside, at a table by the window.

"I'm going to have a toasted sandwich. What will you have?" asked Feruzeh.

"I'll come with you."

"There's no need," she said.

"I'll just have tea," I said.

"Are you sure? Don't you want anything to eat?"

"Maybe later."

Before heading to the bar Feruzeh took a folder full of photocopies out of her bag and put it in front of me.

I looked at the first page: *Impressions of Turkey During Twelve Years' Wanderings*. Under the title it said Professor William Ramsey.

I leafed through the pages.

A big group of people sat down at the next table and started talking at the top of their voices about the old graffiti on the ceiling. They pointed at the pictures of the aeroplanes on the wall, making sure the whole pub heard how fascinating they were.

My attention wandered. Slowly I closed my tired eyes. My mind trembled like a leaf in water.

Feruzeh came back and put the tea tray down on the table.

"Are you tired? Your eyes are red," she said.

"Don't worry, I'm fine. Where did you get this?"

She took the file from my hand.

"I was in the library yesterday. I thought I'd look up travellers to Anatolia for you. That's the first thing I found. I photocopied it."

"There must be some interesting things in here."

"There are. I had a quick look. Ramsey was an archaeologist and he went to your part of the world in the nineteenth century."

She found a page that she had marked earlier. "I think he was the traveller who visited the house of the agha in your grandmother's story. Look '... he entertained us with what he called sherbet, which was only dirty-looking water sweetened with sugar. Sterrett manfully drank his glass, and kept up our credit for decent manners; but I could not get the stuff down', he says."

I read the paragraph Feruzeh was pointing to.

"This is amazing," I said.

The comments of the people at the next table about the Second World War pilots who had gone there and written their names on the ceiling were getting louder and louder.

"I can hardly hear you," said Feruzeh.

"We should shout like our neighbours at the next table."

"Let's go to the library together some time. You might be able to find some other references."

"I'd like to. Did you think of my grandmother's tree in the library as well?" I asked.

"Not me, my mother. When I was telling her your stories yesterday she said the apple tree reminded her of Newton's apple tree. I phoned you straight away."

"Did you tell your mother my stories?"

"Yes."

The barman brought the food and put it on the table.

Without waiting Feruzeh took a bite out of her hot toasted sandwich. Then she asked, "Do you mind my telling my mother?"

"That's not what I meant…"

I put sugar in my tea and stirred it slowly.

Feruzeh stared.

"What's up?" I said.

"I thought you drank your tea without sugar?"

I paused.

"This is what happens when I haven't slept," I said. "Sometimes I don't know what I'm doing."

"Didn't you sleep last night?"

"I don't sleep much. But I don't let it get to me anymore," I said, and took a sip of my sugary tea.

"You should see the doctor if you have insomnia."

"I've been taking every pill in the world for the last ten years."

"And nothing's helped? Ten years is a long time."

"Time is a better healer than medicine."

"My mother had insomnia for a while too, but she recovered. What do the doctors say?"

"They say don't strain your mind, relax. Before, they were worried I might take the final medicine."

"What medicine?" asked Feruzeh, cup in hand.

"One day while I was waiting for the doctor, a patient suffering from the same problem said suicide was the final medicine."

"Was it that bad?"

"When crying doesn't help you bang your head against the wall."

Feruzeh put her cup down without drinking.

"Did it start suddenly?" she asked.

"You could say that …"

"Just like that?"

"After an accident."

"A car accident?"

"An accident with the police. In my country if you're politically active you could end up like your father did."

"You mean they tried to kill you?"

We fell silent.

I touched Feruzeh's cup.

"Your tea is cold," I said.

"It's fine," she said.

Just then her telephone rang. I seized the chance to get up. When I returned carrying a tea tray she had finished talking.

"You shouldn't have, I'm quite happy with cold tea."

"I didn't like my tea with sugar."

"That was my mother. She asked me to get her a couple of things," she said. "I have to go shopping in a bit. She's having a birthday party tonight and she's invited you too."

"Thank you. I'll be there, unless the sleep fairy comes to visit."

I took a sip from my tea.

"We were talking about your insomnia," she said.

"Your mother's birthday is more important," I said. "What can I get her?"

"You don't have to get her anything. But she likes jewellery and antique books," she said.

"Is that the same as you?" I asked.

"When it comes to jewellery, yes …" she said.

I looked at her earrings. Two stones the colour of clotted blood swung on the end of copper filigree. Her necklace was also copper and, like the other day, it had a rose in the centre.

"I've decided what my present is going to be," I said.

"So quickly?"

"Yes."

"It's been years since my mother last celebrated her birthday, but two weeks ago she fell down the stairs and broke her ankle. She wants to get together with her friends."

"What's your mother's name?" I asked.

"Azita."

I tried to pronounce it the way she did, by extending the middle syllable.

"What does she do?"

"She translates books from English into Farsi."

"She must have had plenty of time to translate these past couple of weeks," I said.

"My aunt from London is here looking after my mother. They don't have time for anything except watching television and gossiping."

"Idleness is a delightful sin," I said.

"What are your favourite sins?" she asked.

I pondered the question as I sipped my tea; slowly I put my cup down on the table.

"I can't think of any," I said.

"Are you sinless?"

"No. But I haven't committed as many sins as Tolstoy yet either."

"All right, but are you as determined as he was to purge them?"

"That's an even more difficult question," I said.

"If you answer the easy questions there'll be no need to ask the difficult ones," she said.

"In that case, let me ask is there any one sin that really attracts you?"

"Do you want me to lie?" she replied.

"Yes."

"I'll tell you when I've found out what your sin is," she said.

She sipped her tea.

The drone of all the other tables blended into the racket from the next table.

We left the pub and did Feruzeh's shopping. Then I walked home along the river.

I tried lying down. The sleep fairy didn't arrive.

I left to go to Feruzeh's house as the sun was setting. On the way I met some teenagers painting graffiti. In the underpass beside the shopping centre a thin boy stood on two people's shoulders to reach the top of the wall.

"Do you need any help?" I said, laughing.

"Cheers mate, we're all right," they said.

I wondered if they had painted all the graffiti in the city.

When Feruzeh opened the door I handed her the inexpensive but deep red roses I got from the Co-op. She was wearing her hair loose.

I greeted the first two people I saw in the sitting room. Feruzeh took me to meet her mother who was sitting by the window. I could see the plaster on her left foot under her long dress.

Her mother said my name before Feruzeh had introduced me.

"Brani Tawo ... I believe?" she said.

She hugged me affectionately. My eyes misted over.

I felt as though I were in the home I had left years ago. I had forgotten how that felt.

"Happy birthday," I said.

"Thank you for coming. I know you from the stories you've told Feruzeh," she said.

I blushed. I hadn't expected such warmth.

Azita introduced me to a woman who joined us. "This is Brani Tawo," she said.

Her pronunciation of my name was so charming I could have phoned her every day, just to hear it.

"You're Feruzeh's friend, aren't you?" asked the woman.

"Yes," said Azita. Then, turning to me, she said, "This is my sister Tina."

Tina kissed my cheek gently.

"Just call me aunty like Feruzeh does," she said.

"Okay aunty, I will," I said. We all smiled.

"Has Feruzeh ever played 'Three Word' with you?" asked Tina.

"No," I said.

"Good. We'll play tonight," she said.

Feruzeh had wandered off. I had given her the roses but my gift to Azita was still in my hand.

"This is for your birthday," I said.

"Thank you dear," said Azita, kissing my cheek.

Amalia Rodrigues was playing on the stereo. I went to the buffet table and served myself humus, dolma, cacık, salad, chicken and chips.

Holding my full plate, I met Feruzeh in the kitchen a few moments later.

"What's the 'Three Word' game?" I asked.

Feruzeh laughed. "I see you've met my aunt," she said.

"She seems very sweet."

"Don't forget that word," she said.

"Which word?"

"Sweet."

"Okay," I said.

"What did you buy my mother?" she asked.

"You'll never guess," I said.

"I saw the size of the parcel it can't be jewellery. Is it a book?"

"I'm not telling you," I said.

There were two other women in the kitchen. I greeted them and introduced myself. They were preparing more dishes of fresh fruit. Feruzeh finished cutting the melon she was holding. She put the knife on the edge of the counter.

"I want to know what your present is. I'm going to go and peep."

"Isn't peeping a sin?"

She laughed. "You've still got that on the brain. Clearly you're a great sinner," she said.

Her hand brushed against the knife on the counter. It clattered to the ground, lodging itself between our feet.

One of the women came and picked up the knife and spoke to Feruzeh in Farsi.

"Are you all right?" I said.

"Yes," said Feruzeh.

I could feel her breath.

I put my plate on the counter. "I nearly dropped it," I said.

Feruzeh took a sip from her glass of wine on the counter. Then she passed it to me. "Have some, it will do you good."

"Okay," I said, and shared her drink.

I wasn't really a drinker. But if I had been, I, too, would have preferred red wine.

"Isn't Stella here?" I asked.

"She'll be here soon," she said. "Now go and meet everyone in the living room."

I picked up my plate and went into the living room. I met an English couple who lived on Feruzeh's street. The man worked for the council, the woman was an editor at a London publisher and talked about the Cambridge Word Fest that was due to start in a week's time. A young woman who overheard joined us. She was one of the festival's organizers. While we were discussing literature the subject of writers' eccentricities came up and we were joined by a man with a white beard. Enunciating each word perfectly, like a BBC news reader, he said that in a world where even God demands people's love and attention we shouldn't read too much into this little weakness of writers. We agreed, laughing.

The lights went out and the birthday cake arrived from the kitchen. Azita blew out the candles. We all said "Happy birthday." Then the Iranians sang a song in their own language in chorus. The lights came back on.

I took my plate back to the kitchen. The water in the kettle was hot and I made myself a cup of tea.

Except for a few people, everyone was gathered around the large table. Feruzeh beckoned to me, I went and sat beside her on the large sofa. She had cut me a piece of cake.

Tina's voice was the loudest. It was obvious that she knew everyone there. She had something to say to each guest.

"Let's have a little look at the presents," she said, as though it were her birthday.

Inside the first parcel was a summer shirt. The second gift was an envelope containing a membership card for two people at the Picturehouse cinema.

Azita opened a third parcel at random. Inside was a folder and she read the note on it.

"When did this arrive?" she asked.

"Last week," said Feruzeh. "Aunty and I decided to save it till today."

It was a draft translation into Farsi of Marquez's latest novel. A publisher in Tehran had had it translated from Spanish and, to make sure it didn't get banned, they were asking Azita to compare it with the English translation and, if necessary, make certain inoffensive changes.

We discovered that Azita's excitement was because she had once had the honour of meeting and chatting to Marquez at a gathering and had later exchanged a couple of letters with him.

"I'd like to read this novel in Spanish," she said.

"What's Marquez's English like?" asked the man who worked for the council.

"When I first met him I thought his words were poetry," replied Azita.

Everyone laughed.

"And I still think so," she added.

"Would a Nobel laureate's novel have problems in Iran?" asked the council man.

"I very much doubt that these people who pick bones in Sa'di's *Gulistan* will make any exceptions for Marquez."

"What will you do?" asked the festival organizer.

Azita opened the first page of the file on the table.

"To fit through a small space a cat can squeeze its body until it's as narrow as its head," she said. "Look, the publisher has started out by changing the title: *Memories of My Sad Beauties*."

"A great alternative for *Memories of My Melancholy Whores*," said a man with black-framed glasses.

I had either heard him speak at a conference or seen him working at the market.

"How would you translate it?" asked the editor.

"*An Old Man's Misguided Life*," replied Azita.

"Really?"

"I'll tell you my gut feeling. I'll allow the publisher to have any title they want, but I don't want to change a single word of the story."

The people around the table voiced their approval.

"I haven't read it," said Tina. "Have you got it?"

"Yes," said Azita, and she asked Feruzeh to go and get the book.

Feruzeh put her glass down on the table and went into the next room. I could see through the open door that the walls were lined with bookshelves.

"Before we carry on with the rest of the presents, how about warming up a bit? Let's play the 'Three Word' game," said Tina.

This was the moment I had been waiting for.

The man with the white beard asked, "Who are you going to nominate first?"

I knew Tina would turn sideways and look at me.

"Brani Tawo," she said, "will you describe me in three words?"

"But I've only just met you," I said.

"First impressions are important. They liven the game up," she replied.

Everyone was looking at me. Feruzeh was in the other room looking for the book.

"Sweet," I said.

There were murmurs of approval. I thought about the next two words.

"Sociable and sensitive."

"Where did you get sensitive from?" asked the man with the black-framed glasses. I think he had a stall in the market.

Everyone laughed.

"He's right. I could tell immediately that he was intelligent," said Tina.

I thought I had got off lightly.

"Now describe yourself in three words," commanded Tina.

"Melancholy," I said immediately.

"Are you really?" she asked.

"Yes he is," replied Azita instead of me.

"Sleepless," I said for the second word.

"Objection," chorused the people around the table on the grounds that that wasn't part of my personality but an everyday problem. If we had played this game yesterday I couldn't have given that response. I didn't tell them that sleep deprivation had become a fundamental part of my being, that it had changed my whole life, my relationships, even my character.

Feruzeh returned. Handing the book to her mother she said, "It's true, he has insomnia."

The table fell silent. No one protested.

"Go on," said Tina.

I thought. I couldn't think of the last word.

"Sinless," said Feruzeh.

I was about to object, but then realized I would have to accept it if I wanted to get the game over with. "Sinless," I repeated.

The man with the black-framed glasses said, "We can't prove he's not."

He may have been the man who gave a speech in the church where I met Feruzeh. He might not have been wearing his glasses that day.

After debating a few ideas the committee around the table declared my answers to be acceptable.

Just as I was about to breathe a sigh of relief Feruzeh whispered, "Ask someone else straight away."

But the festival organizer beat me to it.

"What three words would you use to describe me?" she asked.

As if sleep deprivation wasn't punishment enough.

Azita suddenly told the man beside her, very loudly, "This isn't the book that Marquez wrote."

I realized it was a ploy to save my skin.

"How so?"

She stepped in to answer the inquisitive questions, thus putting an end to the game.

Azita told us what had happened during the publication of *Memories of My Melancholy Whores* three years previously. Apparently, while the book was still at the printers it fell into the hands of pirate publishers, who released it onto the market. The whole world was awaiting the book with great anticipation as it was Marquez's only novel in the past ten years and possibly his last. Furious with the publishers, Marquez stopped the publication, made some changes to the end of the novel and published the amended version.

"Interesting," said the man with the white beard. "So the real version is the one the pirates have?"

"Of course not, the real book is always the writer's final version," said Azita.

"The changes weren't in the true spirit of the book; he made them to get the pirates back. The real version was the one the pirates published. That's the one I would have liked to read," said the man with the white beard.

"If this isn't the real version I'd better not read it," said Tina.

"Don't be silly …" protested Azita.

The table turned into the ten-minute pause at conferences. Everyone started talking at once.

Seeing as the pirates had got hold of the real version then they owned the true one. No, the pirates' stealing the book was like the Devil meddling with the truth. The writer's subsequent changes to the book were necessary for its own good. But no, the Devil had defended God in spite of God, warning that God – who should have no equal – would undermine Himself by creating people in His own likeness. The pirates were now defending the book against the writer.

"Have you read it?" asked Feruzeh.

"Yes," I said.

"What did you think of it?"

"The man in the novel listened to Bach's cello suites in his house. I had a fantasy about writing a novel with Bach's suites in it. When I saw that he had got there before me I stopped reading. I couldn't touch it for two days."

The argument around the table continued.

People are God's utopia. That's why God breathed His own breath into them. No, it wasn't God who created utopia, it was people. People had no choice in being created, but they could decide how to live their lives. That's why the first woman, the mother of all humanity, ate the forbidden fruit.

That's why the realm of existence where she ended up is people's utopia.

"It's against God's rules," said the man with the black-framed glasses, "but people reach utopia by crossing the forbidden line. The writer objects too, but it's only by violating prohibitions that pirates can get their hands on the real book." He was probably a university lecturer.

They gave the floor to Azita to round up the debate.

"Everyone who upsets my Marquez is evil," she said.

The table fell silent.

Feruzeh leaned towards me and said, "You can write your novel without Bach's suites."

"No matter what I put in their place, I'll still feel there's something missing in the story," I said.

Feruzeh took the plate from my hand.

"Will you have some more cake?"

"No thank you," I said. "My head is aching so much I can't open my eyes."

"I'll make you a coffee."

"I should go home and lie down."

"But the night is still young ..."

"Any minute now they'll start playing the 'Three Word' game."

"I'll protect you," she said.

As I was standing up I asked, "Who's the man in the black-framed glasses?"

"The Irish man? His name's O'Hara," she said. "He's a born revolutionary, like you."

"What does he do?"

"These days his main occupation is writing love poems to my aunt."

"Good for him," I said.

"But my aunt is playing hard to get."

We went into the kitchen. Feruzeh packed me some cake and home-made cookies.

"You can eat these tomorrow," she said.

"Thank you."

"Would you like some more?"

"This is plenty," I said.

Azita came in.

"Are you leaving?" she asked.

"I couldn't sleep last night; I'm tired," I said.

"I can see from your eyes."

"Thank you for everything. I'm very pleased to have met you."

"What did your fortune say?"

"What fortune?"

"Didn't Feruzeh tell you your book fortune?"

"No," Feruzeh and I said together.

"This is your first visit to this house," said Azita. "I don't want you to leave without hearing your book fortune."

Feruzeh went to fetch the book.

"When we were young girls Tina and I used to tell our fortunes all the time. We each had a book. We would open a page at random. Whichever poem it happened to be was our fortune," said Azita.

"You still tell them …"

"Of course," she said.

Feruzeh came back holding the book with the rose design that I had seen at the pub the other day.

"This is your 'book of secrets' …" I said.

"Yes," said Feruzeh.

She handed me the book and told me to choose a page.

I placed my finger inside. Mother and daughter looked at the page I had opened together.

Azita asked, "Have you ever been to a graveyard here?"

"No," I said.

"The dead are good for all eternity. If you visit them you will see the eternity inside yourself," she said.

Then she hugged me and hobbled slowly out of the kitchen.

"Do you know Forough? That was one of her poems," said Feruzeh.

"I don't know her," I said.

"She's one of our women poets. She died young."

"Is that why your mother mentioned a graveyard?"

"It may have been in a line in the poem."

"Do you like the poem?" I asked.

"I know it by heart."

Feruzeh touched the words with her slender fingers. Slowly she translated it.

Another song was starting in the living room.

5
ANCIENT İSMAIL

Those Seeking their Way in the Darkness

The night that Tatar the photographer arrived, the villagers chatting at Kewê's house were more concerned about Ancient İsmail than about the Claw-faced woman's two daughters who were nowhere to be seen. The girls would eventually return from their giddy rambles, but Ancient İsmail, who shepherded sheep alone, did not stay out on the moorlands late at night like the young shepherds and he was usually home by now. Tatar the photographer said that on his way from Mangal Mountain a young boy had asked him about Ancient İsmail. Everyone was anxious.

Some twenty years earlier, at the end of the war, the only people who inhabited the villages were women, children and the elderly. It was silent everywhere; all the houses were abandoned. Ancient İsmail was sixty years old and all the conscripts had given him everything they owned for safe keeping, from their sewing needles to their patterned rugs. A group of bandits got wind of the fact and descended late one night like hungry wolves in the snow, when the full moon was at its zenith and the villagers were asleep. It was 'open sesame': there are secrets capable of moving every stone, a key capable of unlocking every lock. The bandits went to the barn first and woke the boy who was sleeping with the ewes who were about to lamb. Holding the gun against his head, they dragged him to the front door of the house. The boy called out, "Father, open the door." "What's up?" said İsmail.

"One of the ewes has lambed, it's cold out here, let's bring her inside."

Ancient İsmail said, "Don't worry, just tuck it under the straw."

The boy insisted. Just at that moment, İsmail's young wife said, "I didn't bolt the door, it's open," the ground shook and the men surged in like an angry river. Snowflakes, the howling wind and a breathless fear enveloped the house.

İsmail told them to take anything they wanted as long as they didn't touch the women. One of the men started to light the gas lamp, but Ancient İsmail stopped him, saying, "Don't light the lamp, I don't want to see your faces." They tied İsmail's hands and searched the house for gold and silver in the dark, but found none. They asked İsmail where he had hidden the entrusted treasure, but he gave no answer. The men took İsmail's four-month-old baby girl from his second wife outside. They laid her down on the snow like a lamb and held a knife against her throat. The full moon shone onto the baby's face and, after screaming once, she lost her tongue as though she had fallen into a mirror. Sensing his baby's destiny, Ancient İsmail told them that all the treasure entrusted to him was in the old well. The bandits went to the back of the house and lifted the stones covering the well, before removing the branches inside it. As they lifted out each rope-bound bundle the bandits panted like wolves dripping blood from their fangs.

At the end of two days during which she did not cry, the baby who lost her tongue in the light of the full moon surrendered her life. Ancient İsmail buried his baby, saddled his emaciated horse and went to the town of Haymana. At the recruiting office, which had re-opened once the war had ended, he wept as he reported the bandits that had invaded his house and told them of his baby that had abandoned her innocent soul.

Just as the captain was about to tell him to wait for a few days, news arrived of the capture of a band of robbers.

Two hundred years earlier the French botanist Tournefort had written in his travel diary that, unlike Turkmen bandits, Kurdish bandits did not attack at night. But, with the wars, taxes and destitution that marked the times, the darkness of the night had made itself indispensable to every bandit. Two nights after Ancient İsmail was attacked the bandits had gone down into a storehouse in a nearby village filled with bales of wool and angora, entering by knocking down the adobe wall. The bandits, who dragged a bundle of twigs behind them to ensure they didn't leave any tracks in the snow, didn't realize that an oleaster bundle had a hole in it. When they awoke the next morning the elderly male villagers strapped on their guns and, foraging in the snow, followed the trail of the oleaster berries. At midday, they reached a stream at the bottom of Mangal Mountain and found seven men asleep, wrapped up in their rugs. Having taken away the gun from beside each of the men, they woke them up by firing a bullet into the air. The old men went to the town of Haymana the following day, with seven bound bandits in tow and a crowd of children in their wake, and entered the recruiting office.

The commander asked Ancient İsmail if he knew the bandits. İsmail told them he had not seen their faces in the dark but that he would be able to recognize the man who had tied him up, from his fingers. They lined up the bandits and İsmail touched each of their hands in turn. One of them was just a boy and as beguiling as the light of the moon. İsmail touched him as though touching the fingers of the bandit who had tied his hands that night and said, "These are the hands that tied me." The young bandit was called Lille. He was just seventeen, his breath was as fresh as a rose and his face shrouded by an orphan's shadow.

As the soldiers were taking the seven bandits to jail, the prisoners shouted and created a scene. Seizing the opportunity,

Lille escaped to the ruins of the ancient Greek church. There he jumped onto a horse and, dodging the bullets whizzing past him, managed to shake off the cavalrymen pursuing him. For a week he travelled on secluded tracks and, late one night, when he was about to expire from cold and hunger, he reached his village. Wrapped in velvet-lined woollen quilts he lay burning with fever for two days. One day at around noon news came that soldiers had been sighted in the plain. Immediately the women set up their tandoor ovens, placed the gold and silver the bandits had looted over the months inside and covered them with a layer of stones and chaff for burning. They made dough, rolled out pastry and started singing. Lille put on women's clothes, donned a kaftan and started churning buttermilk. With his heavily kohled eyes and the small beads he attached to his muslin there was none more beautiful than he in the village.

The soldiers searched high and low but found neither the gold nor Lille. As a young soldier was shyly eyeing the women's lovely faces and hennaed fingers he suddenly realized that only one woman's fingers did not have henna. The soldier held the un-hennaed hands. Lille sighed and his heart ached like a young branch struck by a knife. A red breeze caressed his skin before racing on. The air resounded with the women's cries, entreaties and reverberating screams.

Lille was sentenced in Haymana. He would pay with his life, by hanging from the end of a rope, for the death of the baby who had died of fright. Lille's sisters and aunts brought the hidden gold and laid it all at Ancient İsmail's feet. Clutching his hands they knelt before him, weeping. If Ancient İsmail forgave him the soldiers would retract the death sentence and the women's only male relative to have survived the war would return to life. But İsmail had not forgotten the scream of his tiny baby suspended from the full moon on the night of the attack. His heart turned to ice and froze; it did not soften like snow that melts in the sunshine.

Lille was brought to the scaffold. Tradition being immortal, they granted him a last wish. At his request, instead of a holy Qur'an they gave him a reed pipe. Lille played a timeless steppe melody to the crowd gathered in the square, the children watching from a distance and the starlings pecking for food in the snow.

Hush and listen, the wind will tell you which dream is quickly shattered and
Which dream people come back to, hush and listen, the wind will tell you,
Roses bloom, the wind blows softly,
To the enamoured youth gently,
After a lifetime spent broken on a bird's wing
What do people yearn for in their last breath, hush and listen, the wind will tell you.

Lille's sisters married men who returned from the war, vowing to bring not children but swords of vengeance into the world. They named the first male child in the family 'Lille' in memory of their brother. When the new Lille turned seventeen they strapped a gun to his waist and sent him to find Ancient İsmail.

Lille set off, asking pedlars, shepherds and Tatar the photographer, whom he met on the way, for directions. When at noon he found Ancient İsmail he stopped, raised his head and gazed up at the sky. A drop of blood oozed from his lip that had cracked in the midday sun. Lille repeated his name as though making a sacred vow and, drawing his gun in the merciless steppe, he pulled the trigger. But destiny had its own account in Haymana Plain and the life of every Lille flowed into the same river. The gun jammed. "Go away from here," said Ancient İsmail. "One death is enough to destroy a life." Lille did not listen to him but, seizing his knife, attacked like a hungry wolf descended from the mountain. Ancient İsmail was strong despite his years and he plunged his own shepherd's knife into the young boy's heart. Dogs barked, the larks took flight. If this Lille had killed him Ancient İsmail would have been released from the pain of that other death too. The realization hit him as he lay enfolded in his rug until nightfall, convulsed with tears, burning with fever and shaking as though in the throes of epilepsy.

He knew he had to get rid of the corpse and dump it in the creek in the south before daybreak. As it was growing dark Ancient İsmail hoisted the body onto his shoulders. At the bottom of Mangal Mountain he set off first in the direction of the east, then of the south. To avoid the shepherds who watched by night he took secluded routes, wading through stream beds. As he put the corpse down beside a rock to catch his breath, he heard laughter ringing out in the darkness. He tiptoed in the direction of the laughter and peeped. He saw Ferman sitting by a freshly dug grave, with two girls before him laughing and dancing. They had lit a bonfire. Ancient İsmail, consumed by grief for the boy's untimely death, recognized Ferman through his misty eyes, but did not realize that the others were the Claw-faced woman's twin daughters. He took them for two fairies that had taken on the form of girls. He imagined that as they had dug a grave they were waiting for a dead body, maybe they knew that Ancient İsmail had killed a man.

When Ancient İsmail arrived at the creek after midnight he was soaked in sweat. He hid the corpse among the reed beds and washed his hair and neck with water he poured from his cupped hands. For years he had performed his prayers twice, once for himself and once for the executed Lille, but his prayers were not strong enough to bear a new death. He would in any case pay for the sin in the afterlife. This soil, this sky, could not heal the wound of an old man. Before returning to his herd he lay down on the ground, breathing deeply, and looked up at the bright sky. The stars were swaying gently, the moonlight dripped like weary water. The herds' bells and a shepherd's reed pipe could be heard from the mountain top.

Just then lightning struck, like a dagger that glints suddenly in the darkness and vanishes. A scream rang out from the summit of the hill and İsmail stood up and searched the infinite skies from east to west. He had no idea where this lightning had come from on this summer night. Panting, he climbed to the top of the hill. When he reached the plain he saw that the sheep had dispersed and the dogs were waiting beside a shepherd lying on the ground. The shepherd, who was not moving, had been struck by lightning and his left side was completely black. The smell of charred flesh pervaded the air.

They had heard the lightning strike in the village too, but the thought that a tragedy might occur hadn't crossed anyone's mind. A handful of people were searching for the Claw-faced woman's daughters in the village barns. The neighbours at Kewê's were discussing who the young boy who had asked Tatar the photographer about Ancient İsmail might have been. Tatar said that when he had taken his photograph the young boy's teeth were clenched and that he had a piercing, razor sharp look in his eyes. He would develop the photo when he returned to the town, but it wasn't until he brought it the following year that Ancient İsmail recognized the face. When, one year later, he encountered once again the image of the boy he had killed, Ancient İsmail thought Azrael was playing games with him and lay awake the entire night, before surrendering his life at daybreak.

6
WITTGENSTEIN

All Souls Lane

S lowly I half opened my eyes.

I thought of the words of the poem Feruzeh had read the night before: "Let's believe in the beginning of the cold season."

The pain in my head made it impossible to get out of bed. I drifted back to sleep.

A good while later I woke up to the sound of banging. It was midday.

My long, exhausting sleep had once again been dreamless.

I had a shower.

I had tea with bread and butter, cheese and jam for breakfast.

I glanced out of the window. There was no sign of yesterday's spring weather. Clouds shrouded the sky.

As I was going out I looked at the photograph on the wall. Juliette Binoche saw me off with her innocent gaze. It was comforting to think there was someone at home waiting for me.

I didn't take my bicycle, I felt like walking.

I walked down to the river path and felt the cool air reviving my skin as I breathed it in. The joggers along the river and the rowers had started their day long before me.

I walked quickly as far as Bridge Street but I was more sparing with my breath going up the slope. I stopped when I reached the cul-de-sac halfway down Huntingdon Road.

There was a sign on the wall saying "All Souls Lane". It was a good name for a street with a graveyard.

I knew there was a small graveyard attached to the church but until today I had never thought to go and explore it.

The left side of the road was lined with trees. I walked slowly along the narrow path.

In one house I heard an alarm clock go off four times.

I saw the man sitting at the window. He stared at me with the look of old men who know the fate of the seasons. His long hair floated down to his shoulders, like dead leaves.

I walked towards the church. I reached the first graves.

I knew Wittgenstein was buried there.

Wittgenstein, who bore death on his forehead like an angry scar, did not choose suicide like his brothers. Fixated as he was with the other world during his lifetime, he waited for his appointed time to come.

On the right, two men were digging a grave. I greeted them.

"Do you know where Wittgenstein's grave is?"

The freshly dug earth was soft, ready to receive the newly dead. I remembered Ancient İsmail's fear in the darkness of Haymana Plain all those years ago at the sight of a freshly dug grave.

"Was he buried here recently?" asked one of the men.

"He's been dead for over fifty years."

The hands of the other gravedigger holding the spade had turned red with cold. His bones protruded.

"Was he a philosopher?" he asked.

"Yes."

But that's not what Wittgenstein wanted to be known as. Sometimes he was a communist, sometimes a racist and some-times an Italian prisoner of war. He believed he was a great sinner and used to say that God, whom he likened to an evil judge, would never spare him.

The gravediggers didn't know that. They were busy digging graves for dead bodies in this garden where every soul would end up eventually.

"Yes, he was a philosopher," I confirmed.

The gravediggers stopped working for a moment. They stuck their spades into the soil.

"A woman was asking about that same grave this morning," said the older one.

I wondered if it might have been Feruzeh. Last night when Azita was telling me to go and visit the dead I thought of this grave. But I didn't remember mentioning it to Feruzeh.

"What did she look like?" I asked.

"She was a middle-aged lady in a white coat holding a bunch of roses."

A row of freshly dug graves were waiting expectantly, like hungry children.

"Are you a philosopher as well?" asked the younger grave-digger.

My foot slipped, I narrowly missed falling into the grave. They just managed to grab my arms and pull me back.

"Don't rush to go to your grave."

We laughed as though we were at a fun fair instead of a graveyard.

The last time I had been to a graveyard was to bury a friend. The old people weeping in the rain while various young people chanted slogans reminded me of a black and white film. That morning when we had gone to collect his body from the morgue, I had looked at the complexion that young girls had loved so much, but all the rosy colour was drained from his face. It was impossible to count his wounds. Bullet holes were planted all over his body like kisses, from the centre of his forehead to his feet.

"I'd quite like to live a bit longer," I said.

"Who for? For yourself or for your children?" asked the older gravedigger.

"I don't have any children."

"You live for yourself then."

"Some of my friends died young. I want to live for them."

"That's not how philosophers talk," said the young grave-digger. "I could tell you weren't a philosopher."

"Can't philosophers have dead friends then?" protested the older gravedigger.

"They don't think of the dead as part of life."

"Oh, and you reckon philosophers think of anything other than death?"

"They worry about death," said the young gravedigger. "But they don't care about the dead."

"How can you talk like that before you've had a single beer?"

"If you buy the beers tonight I'll show you."

"Why don't you come with us mate, we're going to The Eagle tonight," the older gravedigger said to me.

"All right but I won't have beer, I'll have something else."

"Why?"

"Don't you get it? He's a Muslim," said the young gravedigger.

"I've got loads of Muslim friends; they drink more than I do," said the older gravedigger.

"Then they pray all night."

We laughed.

I didn't tell them I had drunk wine last night. Neither did I mention that fog had obscured the bridge between myself and God. Wittgenstein had said that what we cannot speak about we must pass over in silence. I accepted the cigarette that the older gravedigger offered me. I drew the pleasure of smoking in a graveyard in the cold into my lungs. I coughed.

"Is this philosopher of yours a Muslim?" asked the older gravedigger.

"No," I said.

"How can you have a Muslim philosopher?" asked the younger gravedigger.

The older gravedigger grew serious: "That's taking the joke too far."

"I'm not joking, I'm telling the truth. Have you ever heard of a Muslim philosopher?"

The older gravedigger paused and thought for a while.

I looked at the younger gravedigger.

"You name me a Christian philosopher and I'll name you a Muslim one."

We each took a drag from our cigarette.

A few drops of rain fell.

"I hope we don't get caught in the rain," said the younger gravedigger.

"Don't change the subject," said the older gravedigger.

"I can't think of the names of any philosophers," said the younger gravedigger. "You're a Christian, you help me."

The older gravedigger scratched his head. He looked at the open grave. "I know a philosopher," he said. "The Pope."

They tittered with laughter like children. I thanked them for the cigarette.

"I'd better go and look for Wittgenstein," I said.

"The old graves are on the other side of the church," said the older gravedigger.

"What do you want to find him for?" asked the younger gravedigger. "All graves are the same."

"What do you mean?" asked the older gravedigger.

"Each dead body is separate, but the souls of the dead all join together."

"All right, the beer's on me tonight. That was impressive."

"Cheers."

"But because our two souls are joined together I can drink yours."

"Not while we're alive," said the younger gravedigger. "Our souls can't join together before our bodies have died."

"Where did you get that from?"

"My granddad started talking like that when he got dementia."

"He must have been getting ready to die then," said the older gravedigger.

When I was at university my friends and I used to play a game called "Who's the best dead person?" We would name three characteristics. We would start off with a film, a goodbye letter or a word we heard in the street. The characteristics would change every day and we would have to find dead people to suit them. We would say Deniz, Spartacus or Leyla. Death's eternity had shrouded them all in a shared destiny. We too were ready to die, but we didn't know which of us would be the first to join that caravan. "I'll buy you a beer tonight," I said to the younger gravedigger.

"And I'll do you a favour in return."

"Just learn a few philosophers' names, that will be enough," I said.

"All right, deal."

Anyone would think the two gravediggers were digging holes for sapling trees instead of for dead bodies. Contact with the soil and the time spent with it brought a freshness to their hearts. Wittgenstein, who knew that, gave up teaching to work in a churchyard as a gardener.

We became absorbed in the peace emanating from the stones, the trees and the gravestones. There was silence. Then a harsh wind blew past us.

The gravediggers told me their names, I introduced myself and we parted after arranging to meet in the evening.

"The dead are good for all eternity," I said as I walked away. "When we are with them we will see the eternity inside ourselves."

"Hey," said the younger gravedigger. "Are you a philosopher or what?"

"You can decide that tonight over a beer."

"Don't worry about sinning mate, you have a drink too. Drunks are as innocent as the dead."

I had no intention of spoiling the taste of the wine I had drunk from Feruzeh's glass last night.

The rain suddenly grew heavier.

I opened my umbrella.

I examined each of the gravestones behind the church in turn. I wandered amongst carved marble, plain gravestones and Celtic crosses.

The graves of young people and children rubbed shoulders with the graves of the old. Death was the same distance away from everyone.

Some gravestones were worn, some overturned, the writing on them no longer legible.

The graveyard was overrun with weeds. I reached the wall on the west side with great difficulty.

As I turned to look at the church I saw the woman in the white coat by the gravestones. She was crouched beside a grave in the downpour.

I knew I had found Wittgenstein.

I coughed gently.

The woman in the white coat raised her head and looked at me.

"Are you dead or alive?" she said.

"Alive."

"How can I believe you?"

"Do the dead cough?"

"Your voice is deep and hazy."

"That's because it's cold. I don't think the dead carry umbrellas either."

The rain had soaked her hair. The hem of her coat was buried in the mud.

I crouched beside her and put my umbrella over her head.

"I'm certain you're not dead," I said.

"How?"

"You're cold. Your hands are shaking with cold."

"It wasn't easy to find this grave," she said.

It wasn't at all easy to find. There was no gravestone above it, just a flat stone lying on the ground. It was covered with mud and pine needles.

The red roses strewn over it were soaked, like the woman's hair.

At the head of the grave was a tiny ladder the size of an outstretched hand, which had been placed there by unknown scholars. Several coins were scattered around it.

"You're all wet. If you stay here any longer you'll get ill," I said.

Black clouds and rain cloaked the sky.

"My pain hasn't gone away yet," said the woman.

"What are you hoping will make your pain go away? The rain, or Wittgenstein?"

She picked up a rose from the grave and held it in the palm of her hand.

It was clear that tears were pouring down her face along with the rain.

"My husband left me yesterday," she said.

I didn't know what to say.

"Catching cold at Wittgenstein's grave won't do you any good," I said.

"Do you believe in fate?" she asked.

"Only in matters of love."

"I'm sure you must be right."

"Did Wittgenstein believe in fate?" I asked.

"I don't know," she said.

"Why are you here then?"

"Perhaps Wittgenstein who knows about today, will know about tomorrow too."

"Is that possible?" I asked.

"Yesterday was our wedding anniversary. I was getting some books down from the bookshelf so I could choose a poem and I dropped one on the floor. I read the line on the open page: 'It is a hypothesis that the sun will rise tomorrow, and this means we do not know whether it will rise.' I looked at the cover; it was Wittgenstein's philosophy book. I'd bought my husband a lovely card. I quoted those words and added: 'I can't be sure of the sun but I'm certain of our love.'"

The woman's voice was trembling.

"Last night my husband didn't come home," she continued. "His phone was switched off. It was only later that I saw the letter he had left on his desk. It said he was in love with someone else, that he'd been meaning to tell me for ages but didn't know how to do it. I looked in the wardrobe; he'd taken all his clothes too."

She crushed the rose in her hand and started sobbing.

"Pain too has a limited life, dear lady; you'll feel better soon," I said.

She took my arm and laid her head on my shoulder.

Azita was right in saying the dead were good for all eternity.

The dead didn't know what evil was, they didn't hurt anybody, but lovers did.

"I'm dead too now. My life is over," said the woman.

"When I was little my aunty got sick," I said. "She used to tell the children who went to see her that she would be dead soon. 'You have a long life ahead of you, make the best of it,' she said. The following day there was a storm and one of the children was carried away by a flood. My aunt is still alive."

"I'm that child carried away by the flood."

"You shouldn't make such sweeping statements about yourself when you're not even sure if the sun will rise tomorrow."

She raised her head and looked at me.

I smiled. She tried to smile too but her eyes, worn out with crying, wouldn't let her.

"Shall I read you a poem?" I said.

"I always carry my book around with me now." She took Wittgenstein's *Tractatus* out of her coat pocket. "Read me something from this."

"You're like Wittgenstein," I said.

"Really?"

I saw her eyes light up for the first time.

"He found a book when he was in the war and he too carried it everywhere with him."

"A poetry book?"

"No. Tolstoy's *The Gospel in Brief*."

"I've never heard of it."

"Wittgenstein found it in a bookshop during the First World War. Because of the war that was the only book left in the bookshop. Wittgenstein interpreted it as a sign of fate. He wouldn't be parted from the book, it was like God was inside those words."

"I thought he was an atheist."

"He was when he was going to war."

"He changed in the war then …"

"I'll tell you the story of a soldier who didn't believe in God," I continued. "About a hundred years ago, when the Greek army that invaded us was defeated they left many dead and prisoners of war behind. Some soldiers asked the villagers to shelter them so they wouldn't be taken prisoner. One of them stayed in our village and changed his name. Although the Muslim villagers accepted him they made fun of him for being a

66

Christian. One day the soldier couldn't stand it anymore. 'Don't mock me,' he said, 'I'm not a Christian, I don't believe in God.' No one had ever seen such fear in a village that had existed for many centuries, not even when the enemy invaded. For days everyone locked themselves in their houses. Eventually they came out and said to the soldier, 'Christianity is fine too, only don't be Godless.'"

The rain suddenly stopped.

"I believe in God," she said.

"In that case He will help you."

"You're very optimistic …"

"Look, it's stopped raining. That's a good sign," I said.

I folded my umbrella. Above us the sky opened like a giant window.

"What does Wittgenstein's book say?" she said.

I opened a page at random. I read the first sentence that caught my eye.

"The world of the happy man is a different one from that of the unhappy man."

The rain had tired us out. We breathed deeply.

"This morning I wanted to die here, but now I want to be healed," she said.

"You will be healed."

I took my handkerchief out of my pocket and dried the woman's face. She was like a helpless child. Her hands were trembling.

"Why did you come here? Are you unhappy too?"

"I came to listen to the eternal breath of the dead," I said.

"Why?"

The sky that was leaden only a few moments ago was starting to clear.

"The clouds are clearing," I said.

"Why?"

"The rain got tired …"

"Not that, I was asking what brought you to this graveyard."

"When you're inside a situation you can't understand it completely. To see all of it you have to step outside it."

"And this is outside it?"

"I think so."

"The dead are outside of life and you came here to understand life, is that right?"

"Being with the dead makes us more aware of life, not death," I said. "We can't attain the meaning of existence without getting close to non-existence."

"Can the dead attain?"

"I hope so …"

"What if they can't?"

"Then we will have missed our chance of understanding this world."

"Is that why people know themselves less than anyone else?" she said. "Because we can't look at ourselves from the outside …"

"We tend to understand others better than we understand ourselves. Knowing ourselves is only possible through the eyes of other people anyway. Other people are our mirrors," I said.

"And we're each other's mirrors too now, aren't we?"

"The real reason we're here is to see the mirror that we can both look into at the same time."

"Which mirror?"

"The one under this gravestone."

We both looked at the gravestone in front of us.

"What a magical thing death is," said the woman.

I started to feel dizzy. My eyes became blurred.

"Death isn't the opposite of life, but its mirror," I said.

"I realized …" she said calmly.

"Everyone realizes it but they can't form it into an idea."

"Not that; what I mean is that when you arrived I realized you were dead. You speak like part of the other world."

I laughed.

"I came from the other world to help you," I said.

"A week today it's the anniversary of Wittgenstein's death. Will you come back then?"

"Whenever Wittgenstein calls, I come."

"Is that so?"

"You won't need me anymore. Your pain will soon be healed," I said.

"I'm beginning to believe you," she said.

"Me too."

"To believe me ...?"

"I meant I'm beginning to believe myself."

She held my hand, smiling.

"You're a nice dead man," she said.

"You," I replied, "are a nice living lady too."

"Do you have any news for me from the other side?" she asked.

I looked at her. She was serious.

"I've just been with Wittgenstein," I said. "He asked me to tell you this: life is divided into two parts; one is the part already lived, the other the part we haven't yet lived. The important part is the one we haven't yet lived."

"Yes ..."

"Yes."

"May I kiss your cheek ...?" she said.

"It's bad luck to kiss the dead," I said.

As she reached up to kiss my cheek she said, "I'm cursed with bad luck anyway."

The north clouds flowed away as quickly as water. The sky cleared, the world became bright.

Before we stood up we each placed a hand on the gravestone. Our skin became smeared with the mud covering Wittgenstein.

The woman in the white coat took my arm.

We walked slowly. As we passed the church we looked at the sparrows perched on the gravestones.

The woman held my arm more tightly.

Nobody leaves a graveyard in the same state of mind as they enter.

We returned in company from the road we had taken alone.

As we were returning from All Souls Lane the alarm clock in the house on the left rang out six times.

The man at the window was still watching the world outside. His long hair floated down to his shoulders, like dead leaves.

7
LITTLE MEHMET

The Mirror with the Rose Motif

While the neighbours at Kewê's house were drinking strong black tea and telling stories the Claw-faced woman suddenly burst in, shouting, "Where are my daughters! Find them!" The pallid night slowed down like an ox cart, the dim light of the lamp flickered. Everyone felt their breath falter amid the tobacco smoke, expressions froze. Then they heard Emir Halit's voice wailing outside. Emir Halit was slumped down on his knees outside the front door repeating, "Lightning struck him, lightning struck him."

The darkness of the night pulled you into itself. Emir Halit and my fourteen-year-old father used to watch over sheep at night and descend the star-studded mountain peaks of the south to explore every nook and every hollow of the 72,000 universes. Emir Halit would close his eyes and play the reed flute, while my father lay on the ground gazing up at the infinite heavens. A red breeze blew gently above them. My father drew circles in the air and tried to catch the shooting stars, making the same wish every time. If his wish ever came true he was ready to attribute it to the stars' compassion. The night gave them a loving home. The dogs would stretch out on the ground, the sound of the sheep's bells would gradually die down. The moonlight would drip down like clear water to the accompaniment of Emir Halit's reed flute.

That night, as the stars were gently swaying, a flash of lightning suddenly ripped the sky in half. Like a dagger, a thunderbolt plunged down on my father in the darkness, leaving a cloud of dust and smoke in its wake. My father let out a blinding scream, then lay motionless on the ground. The herd scattered, the dogs didn't know which way to run. The world slid into a dark well. The whole of my father's left side was burned and the smell of charred flesh pervaded the air. A few metres away Emir Halit, whose reed flute had fallen from his hand, inched closer, looking around him. Upon sighting my father's body that smelled of flesh and ashes he fell to his knees, too terrified even to cry. Realizing there was nothing he could do, he left the dogs to guard over my father and ran all the way to the village, streaking like the wind, past slopes, stream beds and nighthawks.

When the villagers got the news and arrived at the hill peak in their horses and carts they found Ancient İsmail with my father. It was not in the nature of shepherds to leave their herds unattended. Ancient İsmail, who had wrapped my father's body in a rug, said, "The grizzly bear tore one of my sheep apart, I followed it here." The villagers lent Ancient İsmail a horse to take him back to his herd by Mangal Mountain. They took my father back to the village in the cart.

When my father opened his eyes two days later, he had no recollection of how he had got from the star-studded hilltop to the room in the village. "What happened?" he asked the old man Os, who was weeping at his bedside. The old man Os said, "You put your herd to graze in the field in the next village, and the *mukhtar* there shot you." No amount of courage was a match for the wrath of the earth and the heavens, but hearts were always ready to challenge the cruelty of humans. The old man Os, who had lied to my father so he wouldn't be afraid, prayed for the first time in many years, and repeated incantations that broke spells. My father went back to sleep. He discovered the truth the following day, when his four-year-old nephew Little

Mehmet woke him by touching his burnt arm. They told him exactly what had happened. My father stayed in bed for months, tortured by nightmares of the earth and heavens heaving and burning.

The news of the adolescent who had been struck by lightning and saved by angels' wings spread all the way to the sacred land of Arabia. A wealthy man came to visit my father on his way back from the pilgrimage to Mecca. The rich man, who passed by our village with his four heavily laden horses and two man servants before returning to the town of Haymana, gave my father dates, "Zamzam" water and a hand mirror decorated with a rose motif. The Zamzam water helped my father to gradually regain his strength, the mirror with the rose motif showed him what he would look like once he was back in full health, and as for the dates, they pleased Little Mehmet more than anyone else. Because the pilgrimage to Mecca was not officially permitted in Turkey people set out in secret, passing by the dark ravines on the border. The villagers gazed at the rich pilgrim from the city as though admiring an ornamented horse, they shared his tobacco and were regaled with tales of his travels. Ours was a village without any rich people, the only hope was that the old man Os would find the treasure he had been hunting for so many years.

When Little Mehmet, who grew up on the plains, was studying in Haymana some years later, the teacher came into the class one day brandishing a foreign newspaper and told the children about a country called America. The newspaper she was holding contained news of two shepherds and 400 sheep in Haymana Plain who had frozen to death during the harsh winter. The children clapped with joy, and the satisfied teacher smiled her approval.

Little Mehmet asked his teacher, who had shown them the *Chicago Daily Tribune* dated 26 November 1953, "Have they heard about this in Arabia too, Miss?"

The teacher replied, "Don't think about the Arabs in the desert. They can't read the letters in this newspaper. And because we too have rejected the Arabic alphabet our worlds are now separated." Little Mehmet was as speechless as the day he discovered that the teacher didn't know about my father, who had been struck by lightning. Until the day he died prematurely of cancer of the blood, he couldn't decide whether he should go first to the place they called America, or to Arabia.

The teacher, whose smell was not from here, but of foreign, alluring places, would arrive each day with a new piece of information for the children, saying, "Ignorance isn't not knowing, it's knowing false information, and we're going to overcome that." Little Mehmet, just like the 400 other pupils who were ready to follow their schoolteachers in adulation, did not understand certain words, but he believed that the teacher knew where he needed to go. One day when his mother came to the school, Little Mehmet told her too. That day, ashamed of his mother's baggy trousers, head scarf and her not knowing Turkish, he ran out of the playground as fast as his legs would carry him and, when she came after him, he threw his arms around her in a secluded nook with a longing more intense than anyone had ever seen. Every child carried his mother's smell with him until he died and remembered it on his deathbed, when breathing his last. But right then Little Mehmet, oppressed under the burden of being neither Turkish nor from the city, did not speak to his mother in Kurdish for fear that someone would hear and tell the teacher. His mother had no choice but to believe that it was for her son's good. They were poor, and ready to cling to a happiness they did not know the name of. Little Mehmet was the first person from the village to have gone to the city to study since Ferman's two brothers, who were now dead. But fate knew something others didn't in Haymana Plain: it was not in his destiny to study and also have a long life.

This was the time when doctors hid the word "cancer" from patients to stop death from tormenting their hearts. The day that Ike Eisenhower, the president of the country which had fascinated him for so long, came to Ankara Little Mehmet started vomiting blood. It was his first year at university. The 700,000 people gathered in Ankara with its population of 500,000 waved the Turkish flag with its single star and the American flag with its forty-nine stars in jubilation. Foreign journalists sent news to agencies of an industrialized, modern and prosperous country on mountainous, barren, brown soil. The excitement of the crowd cheering Eisenhower, who waved to them from the open-topped Lincoln car left over from Atatürk, was beyond description.

The citizens of Ankara, who had spent an entire week scrubbing the city clean, had been anxious when it rained the previous day but, when it stopped the following morning, they had crowded into Atatürk Boulevard in the hope of getting a live glimpse of Eisenhower's laugh. During Eisenhower's tour of three continents and eleven capital cities, including Rome, Tehran and Karachi, a woman in Pakistan named her newborn baby Ike Khan in his honour. But impetuous death didn't even wait for the newborn baby to take its first steps before claiming Little Mehmet's life. Little Mehmet's mother lamented her son's premature demise in Kurdish, called him "My lion" in Turkish and cried most of all because he had departed this life before ever having known the love of a girl. As the poet said:

Oh, hell's blindest door, confounded Satan.
Preserve us from the torment of sin.
Though suffering and death be a certainty,
Let love be our life's sustenance.

No one dared mention the word cancer, referring instead to "it" as though it were a bloodthirsty wolf that would pounce when named.

75

My father too believed that Little Mehmet's life was the price for the life that the lightning had spared and, like everyone else, he joined in cursing "it".

Every death reduced those who were left behind. My father felt it even more keenly when he found his hand mirror with the rose motif amongst Little Mehmet's possessions at the hospital. He picked up the mirror and stared into it as though he would see Little Mehmet reflected there, but all he saw were his own red eyes. He remembered how he and Little Mehmet had played like children who had quarrelled while he was in bed after lightning struck him. Such children did not break off all contact, they still talked, but with objects as their intermediaries. "Hey rosy mirror, tell Little Mehmet I said let's go to the stream."

Little Mehmet would reply, "Rosy mirror, tell my uncle that I'll go wherever he likes once he gets better."

The day that the mirror with the rose motif was the intermediary for my father's and Little Mehmet's conversation, when they melted into it and entered another world, was the day Tatar the photographer arrived to take their photograph. Hearing what he wanted to do, the old man Os ran up and blocked Tatar's path: "I won't allow you to take these children's photograph," he said. If the old man Os had let him take it that day, a photograph of my father and Little Mehmet would exist today. But only their mirror remained. The mirror given to my father by the rich pilgrim who had visited him after he was struck by lightning, which my father had given to Little Mehmet when he was starting university, had now been returned to him by death's hand.

8
BROOKE

The Orchard

Feruzeh and I met in the last street in the south of the city. It looked over the fields that pointed to Grantchester.

"You haven't had breakfast, have you?" I said.

"Of course not," said Feruzeh.

We locked our two bicycles together and leaned them against the fence. Feruzeh was wearing jeans and a burgundy T-shirt.

"Let's see if Grantchester has changed during the winter," she said.

"Last autumn my sister came to visit me. She's the last person I went there with," I said.

"Where does your sister live?"

"In Turkey. She came to see me, as I couldn't go."

"Does she come often?"

"It was the first time we had seen each other in seven years."

"When will you be able to go?"

"It will depend on my legal status ... I don't know ..." I said.

We put on our sunglasses and strolled along the path through the grass at a leisurely pace.

There hadn't been a blemish in the sky since it had cleared the day before. The sun shone warm and bright.

"Were you able to sleep okay?" asked Feruzeh.

"More than okay ..."

"I bet you didn't set foot outside."

"I listened to your mother, I went to the cemetery yesterday."

"So soon?" she said.

"I wonder now why I never went before."

"But it was raining yesterday ..."

"I took my umbrella. I met a woman whose husband had just left her. She was crying in the graveyard."

"Women who weep in graveyards ..." said Feruzeh.

We walked on in silence.

We looked at the large meadow carpeted with red poppies and yellow daffodils.

A rabbit shot out of the grass. It stood in front of an elderly couple approaching us from the opposite direction.

The elderly woman bent down slowly and brought her face close to the rabbit.

When we reached them I bent down too. The woman smiled.

The elderly man, who had remained standing, said to Feruzeh, "What a lovely day."

"It's beautiful," replied Feruzeh.

"Are you going to the orchard?" asked the elderly man.

"Yes."

"My wife and I have done this walk every week for forty years."

"The beauty of ritual ..." said Feruzeh.

"I agree," said the elderly man. "When we were young like you we used to walk on this path and meet elderly couples. Now we're old and we've met you."

"Forty years..." said Feruzeh.

"Listen ..." said the elderly man.

They listened to the meadow and heard the larks.

"These birds, the yellow flowers and the river were all here," said the elderly man.

A kingfisher took flight and flew down towards the river.

"Will you join us for a cup of tea?" asked Feruzeh.

"Ah young lady, it would be too far for us to walk all the way back. But we go to the orchard every Monday morning. If you come early one Monday we can have tea then."

"But today is special," said Feruzeh.

The elderly man smiled. "Are you celebrating the anniversary of the day you met?"

The rabbit turned around and vanished in the long grass.

Holding her arm, I helped the elderly woman to her feet.

"Today is the anniversary of the death of Rupert Brooke," said Feruzeh.

"This morning some young people were paying tribute to him in the orchard," said the elderly woman.

"We're going to pay our own tribute," said Feruzeh.

"Today a certain gentleman read me Rupert Brooke's 'The Soldier'," said the elderly woman, indicating her husband.

They looked at me.

"I'll read it too," I said.

"You should," said the elderly man.

"My grandfather died in the First World War, like Brooke," said the elderly woman.

"Let's not depress these young people with talk about death," said the elderly man.

"You're right," said the woman.

We parted, saying we hoped we would meet again and each went our separate ways.

A punt was heading south on the river at the bottom of the meadow. One girl was guiding with a pole while the other two girls in the punt were singing at the top of their voices: "And a river of green is sliding unseen beneath the trees ..."

Burhan Sönmez

Feruzeh hummed the song. A river of green slid away unseen beneath the trees.

Following the footpath that ran through nettles and corn-fields, we arrived at the orchard an hour later. We went to the café, stood in the queue and bought scones, honey, clotted cream and a pot of tea. Carrying our trays, we went out into the garden and sat at a table by the trees. "I've missed the scones and clotted cream here," said Feruzeh. Shooing the wasps away from the tray, I said, "So have the wasps," and poured the tea.

We cut our thick scones in half and spread them with cream and honey. The pleasure of having breakfast in the orchard together ... Our eyes met as we drank our tea. The taste of tea changed depending on whom you drank it with. The sun filtered down between the branches of the apple tree above us. I opened the brochure I had picked up in the café.

I found the page about Rupert Brooke and read 'The Soldier'. Feruzeh listened to me with her eyes shut. The orchard appeared to expand; several blossoms fell from the branches.

"This is in your specialist area," I said. "How would you interpret the beginning of the poem?" I passed her the brochure, Feruzeh read the opening lines:

"If I should die think only this of me:
That there's some corner of a foreign field
That is forever England."

Feruzeh looked at me.

"Do you think the foreign soil a soldier is buried on is conquered land?" I asked.

"Are you talking about imperial peace of mind?"

"We were discussing it in a seminar I went to the other day," I said.

We thought about Rupert Brooke's grave on an island in the Aegean Sea.

"You could interpret it another way," said Feruzeh. "Every soldier carries his home with him. No matter where he dies the smell of the soil where he was born and grew up goes with him."

There was a big group of people sitting at the next table. Several children were running around playing. One child fell over and started crying. A young woman stood up and helped her up.

"If you were buried here what would this land be to you?" asked Feruzeh.

I paused.

The birdsong grew louder.

"The plot of land where I lie would be transformed into Haymana Plain forever," I said. "A red breeze would blow above me."

I heard the rustling of the branches.

Feruzeh spread a scone with cream and passed it to me.

"Do you know, it was a good job that Brooke got ill and died on the way to the front instead of on the front," she said.

"Why?"

"It spared him the pain of having to kill."

A small leaf floated down onto my lap. I picked it up and put it in front of Feruzeh.

"Who would you say is the greatest war poet?" I asked.

She looked into my eyes.

"Is there a postscript to your question?"

"Rupert Brooke or Emily Dickinson?"

She laughed. "You've read *The Catcher in the Rye*."

"Yes."

"Do you remember the answer in the book?"

I nodded.

"I'll vote for Brooke," she said.

"Because he's our countryman?"

"Maybe. His words mean more to us knowing that he once hung out in this garden with Keynes and that he swam in the river down there with Virginia Woolf on a moonlit night."

The children running around started climbing the tree beside us.

Now it was my turn to ask, "If you were buried here what would this land be to you?"

"I've only ever considered the possibility that I might die somewhere else once. Three years ago, when I decided to go back to Iran. I was really going. I even got a tattoo on my shoulder as a memento of my life here."

"What made you change your mind about going?" I asked.

She hesitated before answering.

"I'll tell you, but not today," she said. "Because what I have to say is about weeping women."

I looked to see her expression.

Feruzeh drained the last sip from her teacup then poured more for both of us.

"What's your tattoo of?" I asked.

"A rose," she said.

"The rose on the cover of your book of secrets ..."

"Sometimes you can find infinite meaning in a single design," she said.

"If you ever go back," I said, "your rose will feel different to you in Iran."

"Will you get a tattoo when you're going back to your country? As a memento from here ..."

"I doubt it."

We turned and looked after hearing curiosity in the voices from the next table.

Some young people were standing under the apple tree a little further ahead. One of them was dressed up as Rupert Brooke. Some young girls in costumes from a century earlier had formed a circle around him. They were reciting poetry in loud voices.

"I think they're repeating this morning's tribute. Shall we join them?" I said.

"In a minute."

"I envy poets more than novelists," I said.

"Why?"

"What they do is no different from magic. They speak the language of an invisible world, like magicians."

Every table was looking at them. The young people reciting had created a vortex with the power to suck everything in the orchard inside it.

"If you ever got a tattoo what would it be?" asked Feruzeh.

"I can't think of one thing that represents my life here ..." I said.

"Is the person who returns the same person as the one who arrived?"

"When I arrived there was a real possibility I would die," I said. "Now I'm like a branch that's beginning to come back to life."

"What you're looking for is simple."

"Is it?"

"The phoenix that rises from the dead."

I pointed at the boy who was playing Rupert Brooke in the centre of the young girls.

"He's the immortal bird of legends. A poet whose poems are still read a century later."

"It's getting crowded," said Feruzeh.

Like ships caught up in a giant maelstrom in the middle of the ocean, everyone was gravitating towards the young people.

"When I was little there was an old man in our village; his tattoo was the first one I ever saw."

"What was it?"

"A grizzly bear."

"A grizzly bear?"

"Didn't I tell you about it?"

"No."

"I'll tell you in the meadow, on the way back," I said.

My wanting to tell stories was a sign of my love. Finding stories was easy, my worry was finding the right words to tell them.

"Shall we play a game now?" said Feruzeh.

"I can see that this obsession with games runs in your family," I said.

She laughed.

"Yes, let's play 'One Wish'," she said.

"Okay."

"Ask me for something. Your wish has to seem tough and difficult but it must be possible. Make sure you remember that rule."

"You start so I'll know how to play," I said.

She thought for a while.

"You will write a novel with cello suites in it ..." she said.

"Okay ..." I waited for her to continue.

"In it you will include a sentence that we have said to each other, and no one except us will know what it is."

"It's possible but hard," I said. "I can write a novel but I don't know whether I'll be able to bring myself to mention the cello suites."

"Your turn," she said.

Without hesitating I said, "You will be a shareholder of this garden."

"What?"

"A few years ago they were going to put buildings here but they were stopped at the last minute. The landowner is now considering selling the land to the public in small plots, to make sure that that doesn't happen in the future. That way no one will be able to touch the orchard."

"A garden that belongs to everyone and to no one … Good idea."

"We can buy this little bit where we're sitting; what do you think?" I said.

She smiled.

"A little voice inside me tells me I should trust you," she said.

"You can jump off the edge of a cliff with your eyes closed if you like; I'll catch you."

Feruzeh hesitated.

"Yes, but have you got any money? I haven't," she said.

"Me neither," I said.

"So what are we going to do?"

"We'll get a loan from the bank."

"Hey revolutionary," she said. "If we start owing money to the bank we'll be engaging with this system."

"Let's engage," I said, "but not with this system …"

We both laughed.

"You like changing the meanings of words," she said.

"I'm as innocent as people who don't only see roses as roses," I said. "Like you."

She smiled.

"I've got a pressed rose inside my book, let's give it to the people reading poetry," she said.

The children playing beside us stretched their arms out wide and spun round and round in the vortex. They blended into the throng around the poetry readers.

"What a coincidence," I said. "These children were here when I came here in the autumn with my sister too."

"It's the kind of place that children like."

"Feruzeh ..." I said.

"Yes ..."

"You also have a sister, don't you? I remember your mention-ing her."

"I have a twin," she said.

She turned her head away.

"A twin?" I said. "I didn't see her on your mother's birthday."

"She doesn't live in England."

I took a sip from my tea.

"Does she look like Juliette Binoche too?" I asked.

Feruzeh looked at me.

She leaned forward, until she was close to my face.

"I purge my sins with you," she said.

Her lips curved into a sorrowful smile, just like Juliette Binoche's.

"Shall we talk about our sins today?" I said.

"No, it's much too nice a day to discuss sins," she said.

Slowly she drew away. She sank back into her large chair.

Several blossoms fell from the apple tree above us.

I took the mirror with the rose motif out of my pocket. Before it used to show me the past, now it was showing me the future.

"This is yours now," I said.

Feruzeh accepted it reluctantly.

"It's your father's mirror isn't it? It means a lot to you."

"That's why I'm giving it to you," I said.

She brought the mirror up to her face. She gazed into it as though tumbling into a well that no one knew about, as though discovering the secret of a clandestine life.

Then she covered it with her hand.

9
THE CLAW-FACED WOMAN
The Innocents' Burden

Before Tatar the photographer came to these parts, wolves, foxes and a grizzly bear roamed Haymana Plain. Houses with cooling walls, dogs awaiting the moment they would bark, and the crystalline spring, abandoned by young brides, would sleep embracing the full moon. Bread was scarce, death too common and occasionally, like wounded water, love gushed with blood.

When the Claw-faced woman's twin daughters found two bear cubs behind the mountain peaks on one of those days when every inch of the plain was sprouting green, new life rippled through the village. They raised the bear cubs on dog swill and shielded them from the malice of inquisitive children. When the dogs' barking intensified at night they knew the cubs' mother was roaming close by the village. The Claw-faced woman told them to set the cubs free. The twin girls cried. One morning they climbed to the hilltop together, released the cubs and watched them amble innocently away. A single night passed. The daughters saw the village children dragging one of the cubs through the streets with a rope around its neck. Before anyone knew it, dogs tore the other cub to pieces on the stream bed.

The twin girls cried even harder and from that day they stopped playing with the other children. The Claw-faced woman chased the savage village children all the way to the other side of the hill. As the children tried to shake her off by jumping into the stream beds or by hiding amongst the reeds, they were unaware that a grizzly bear was searching for her lost cubs. The grizzly bear had been wandering for days among the scent of thyme and sprawling speedwell, climbing up slopes and peering behind rocks, panting. For a mother searching for her babies a single night was longer than the torment of an entire lifetime. The enraged grizzly bear attacked everything in her path, leaving the cadavers of the foxes and wolves she had ripped to pieces in her wake.

When the children, who were hiding without making a sound, suddenly saw the grizzly bear, they ran up to the top of the hill and came face to face with the Claw-faced woman. Grabbing a long branch, the Claw-faced woman shielded the children. First she threw a rock at the grizzly bear and then she waved the branch at it. Scenting its cubs' smell close by, the grizzly bear roared, her pain echoed in the furthest hilltops before returning. She could hear the sound of approaching dogs from below. As the Claw-faced woman turned to look in the direction of the sounds, a blow from the grizzly bear sent her reeling onto the rocks. Gunshots were heard, the dogs came even closer. The grizzly bear took to her heels and disappeared from sight. When they saw the blood stains in the river the villagers thought they had shot the grizzly bear, but when they saw the abandoned carcasses of the two wolves on the path they were perplexed. They feared the grizzly bear's pain that was so great it made her abandon the wolves she had killed on the path, uneaten.

Until that day the Claw-faced woman's name had been Saadet. In the past she would plait her hair in front of the mirror, contemplating her face that was as beautiful as water. Then fate played its hand and life continued its course. Saadet, who was left scarred after the grizzly bear's attack, never again sat in front of a mirror. Living like this for the rest of her life was her ransom for the two bear cubs. At times innocents bore the burden of sinners.

Saadet was born in that distant city Ankara. By the time her lieutenant father was done fighting in the First World War and the Greco-Turkish War she had grown into a young woman. Her father returned with a young sergeant from Istanbul in tow. Saadet married the sergeant from Istanbul, but it wasn't just in Haymana Plain that the waters of the river of time flowed murkily, they flowed murkily in the city too.

His inheritance of corpses and wartime nightmares led the sergeant from Istanbul to taverns, where he got into fights and sank to the depths of isolation endured by the homeless. One night he marched his wife through dim streets to a dilapidated mansion. Realizing she was in the midst of a den of drunks Saadet ran to the window and, without a moment's hesitation, jumped into the bushes and spent the rest of the night hiding in a hollow. The following day she returned to her father's home.

The sergeant from Istanbul pounded on the door of the lieutenant who had once been his commander, demanding his wife back. Every night he raised the neighbourhood from their beds. He had exceeded every limit and his life hung from the edge of a precipice. The night the sergeant from Istanbul, whose tears were long spent, burst into the house raining down bullets, he did not cry. The lieutenant and his wife died, Saadet was wounded and the sergeant from Istanbul joined the list of missing persons. All women shared the same fate and every woman accepted the portion due to her. Saadet decided to go to a certain village of which her father had spoken, and disappear into the anonymity and solitude of Haymana Plain. As the poet said:

> Don't ask the salt it doesn't know, don't ask the soil it doesn't see,
> The women were the first to weep,
> In their bare hands a mirror and a knife.

Don't ask the water it doesn't know, don't ask the leaf it doesn't see.
The women were the first to weep.

One night during the Greco-Turkish war, Saadet's father had been wounded in Haymana Plain and lost his unit. At that time the old man Os was sixty years old and he smuggled the lieutenant he had spotted near the village into his home. Three days later the lieutenant got back on his feet and, though he was wounded, stole out into the dark, followed the sound of gunfire, found his own soldiers and rejoined the war. When the war ended and he returned to his family he was as proud of the cigarette case that the old man Os had given him as he was of his medal. Years later, sensing imminent tragedy, he gave his daughter the cigarette case and told her that when she had nowhere to turn to she should head to Haymana Plain and seek out the old man Os. When Saadet arrived in the village pregnant and distraught the old man Os embraced her and wept harder than he had wept during the war when the entire plain was a bloodbath.

A month later Saadet gave birth to twins and Kewê and Asya became her closest friends. Asya, who lived alone, would sing in the cemetery at night, then drop in to see Saadet's daughters. Sometimes she would take the girls to the cemetery and play with them there, placing crowns of cemetery weeds on their heads.

Asya taught Saadet Kurdish and learned Turkish from her. As she listened to Saadet's tales of cars, gramophones and telephones she could barely believe that the sun had seven colours. She only accepted it once they had looked at the rainbow together one day. She thought history was a book filled with corpses and asked when the new war would begin. Saadet told her she must keep the things she told her to herself and not breathe a word to anyone. "People who live in cities don't know each other," she said.

Asya was afraid: "Why?" she asked.

"The city is very big."

Asya tried to imagine the city but couldn't. "So why do they live there?" When she heard that city folk used a black stone called coal for heat she said, "How can you burn stone?" She thought that cities meant going to remote places, whereas in the village remoteness came to you.

Asya taught Saadet that crows descending in flocks in the spring were harbingers of the news of a harsh winter. And also that the best way to keep mosquitos away from children so they could sleep soundly was smoke from dried cow dung. When a rainbow appeared it meant the foxes were celebrating a wedding, children who jumped over a rainbow could change into whichever sex they liked. Love was a matter of fate, separation patience, death a test, while hope was the only remedy. As she listened to all this Saadet gradually came to realize the difference between the worlds of the village and the city. One grew inwards while the other grew outwards.

As Asya spoke she would sometimes stop and listen to the red breeze outside, hoping Ferman would suddenly appear. She would get up and clean the house and lay freshly laundered covers on the beds, as though she had heard a signal bell in the distance. The following morning, having awoken from a delectable dream, she would tell the young brides by the fountain that she would soon attain her desire. There was no one who didn't love her but many who mourned for her. As folk-songs lamenting her fate went from mouth to mouth she was protective of her unfulfilled happiness. She implored God to grant everyone such intense love, but to make everyone else's fate different. Sometimes she would have fainting fits and declare in her delirium, "I'm going to have a child." The young girls would swear by their elder brothers, while Asya would swear by her late father. She didn't pay heed to people's talk and when nothing was heard of the grizzly bear for a while she didn't set much store by the rumours that Ferman had killed her. "A mother whose cubs have died is an orphan, Ferman wouldn't hurt an orphaned bear," she would say. One season later the story was reversed; this time the villagers whispered the news from one ear to another that the grizzly bear had killed Ferman.

The best thing Saadet learned from Asya was to faint as she did, which allowed her to lighten the burden of the troubles afflicting her mind. Otherwise life would have been too much for her. When she felt dizzy she would take deep breaths and her neck, back and stomach would be drenched in sweat. She would spend one night in that condition and the next morning, feeling rested, she would go out early to the front door. She would face the rising sun. She would feed the birds and kiss the matted hair of orphaned children. She had a lovely voice and would sing city songs to herself. She made every effort to live as though she had been born and bred in the village, but the long winter months oppressed her. Her oppression reminded her of the city and she feared she would one day abandon these parts and go back. That fear continued to haunt her until the day she was maimed by the grizzly bear and became the Claw-faced woman.

10
BRANI TAWO

The Beginning of the Cold Season

For three nights in a row I was lulled by the most delicious sleep. I felt as happy as a newborn baby. Beautiful dreams accompanied me as I closed my eyes and remained with me after I awoke.

But it was short lived.

For the past two days I had not been able to immerse myself in sleep, in the depths of that dark lake.

It was now midnight.

When I couldn't sleep my punishment was not being able to listen to whatever I was listening to, and not being able to see whatever I was seeing. Neither could I understand what I was reading. I was only a few pages from the end of *All Quiet on the Western Front* and I picked up the book after switching off the television. But I could make no sense of the sentences, paragraphs or pages and I kept having to go back to where I had started.

In the end I gave up.

I made myself another cup of the lime blossom infusion I had been drinking for days. I picked up an illustrated novel from the shelf and placed it on my bedside table.

I put on the CD player.

The sound of flutes rang out. It was as though the gently lamenting airs were coming from a distant garden.

I poured myself a cup of tea.

What could be the price that "it" demanded of me? When I couldn't sleep I referred to insomnia as "it", not daring to name it even to myself. It wasn't enough that I had left my homeland, that my blood had been shed, my bones broken, that I was so far away from my mother and father. But "it" was merciless, "it" had returned to exhaust me.

The pain in my head was intensifying.

Headaches were like poverty, they made you desperate.

The four sleeping pills I had taken since the previous day hadn't worked. Sleep continued to evade me and my headache didn't get any better either.

I finished my tea.

I tossed the illustrated novel aside after the second page, switched off the light and got into bed. I pulled the quilt over my head.

That was where the lake of sleep was.

I gazed at the dark water and stepped off the edge of a precipice but I remained suspended in the void. I couldn't fall into the dark lake of sleep and lose myself.

I longed to dive into the depths of the water and never come up to the surface again.

I thought that this was what the secret love of death hidden inside our souls must be like.

I wasn't afraid of two or three days of sleeplessness but of worse, as I had suffered in the past.

I remained for several hours with my eyes closed but my mind wide open.

At times aware of the sounds from the streets, at times aware of the flute tunes, I eventually lost my grip on them and strolled amid endless thoughts that a minute later I couldn't identify.

When I ventured out from under the quilt at ten o'clock the following morning my eyes were about to split in half.

I hadn't slept even for a second.

My eyelids throbbed and my sight was blurred.

I had a shower.

I filled the kettle to make tea.

I walked over to the window and looked at the rain falling outside. Had it started during the night or this morning? I couldn't remember.

My mobile phone had been switched off since the day before yesterday.

Sleep was my sacred treasure chamber. While I was there I didn't want to be disturbed by phone calls from anyone.

When I switched the phone back on I saw the text messages. Two were from Feruzeh. "Where are you?" she said, and "Phone me."

I listened to the three voicemails she had left me.

She said she was leaving for Iran. Her sister lived there and she was ill. Feruzeh had to leave immediately.

The last message was from the airport. She just repeated my name "Brani Tawo" over and over again. In the background I could hear announcements of planes about to take off.

I rang several times. Her phone was switched off.

I had to go to her house.

The few coins I had in my pocket weren't enough for a taxi.

At times like this I felt like knocking down the wall with my head.

I got on my bike and pedalled furiously in the rain. Once, on the riverbank, I fell over. A young couple helped me back on my feet and I replaced the dislocated chain and continued to cycle.

When I arrived at Feruzeh's house I was soaked through. Even my vest was drenched.

I rang the bell and waited.

I rang it again.

I looked at the window, the curtains were drawn.

I knocked on the door. No one answered.

Not a flicker from the curtains.

I looked around, in the hope that someone I knew would pass. The street was deserted.

Azita and Tina couldn't have gone to Iran too. Feruzeh didn't mention anything like that in her message.

I propped my bicycle against the wall and went to the corner shop across the road. I asked for a pen and a sheet of paper and wrote a short note with my telephone number and posted it through the letterbox.

They were bound to call me when they got home.

My bicycle was nowhere to be seen.

I looked up the road. Two people were riding their bikes. The rain and lack of sleep had blurred my vision but I was certain that one of those bicycles was mine. At times like these poor people had no choice but to be certain.

I ran after them, calling out.

They turned around and looked at me.

They were two teenage boys. One of them stuck his middle finger up. The other shouted, "Fuck off back to your own country!"

They had realized immediately that here I was a surplus foreigner.

They turned into a side street.

I ran as far as the top of the road.

There was no one there.

When one trouble came the others rained down after it. Today was my trouble day.

Violent urges possessed me when I couldn't sleep. I was capable of taking my suffering out on those two teenagers.

When I arrived home dripping wet, like a stray dog, I was about to faint with exhaustion, cold and lack of sleep. I jumped straight into the shower. My hands were so cold I could barely turn the shower on. I stayed under the jet of hot water for a long time.

I couldn't stop shivering so I put on a sweater and got into bed.

I picked up my phone; I wanted to hear Feruzeh's voice.

In her messages she said, "Your phone's been switched off since yesterday. Are you ill?" And, "If I knew where you lived I'd come and see you."

I listened to the same messages over and over again.

Eventually I imagined myself in Feruzeh's position repeating "Brano Tawi" over and over again when she called me from the airport.

A very long time ago an Eastern master, after spending all night writing about a butterfly, believed he was that butterfly and felt compassion for the master who had stayed up writing by candlelight all night depriving himself of sleep.

I too found myself enmeshed in Feruzeh's desperation and fear as she tried over and over again to reach me in the last hours before her departure. I was desolate, both for her and for myself, for whom she was concerned.

I dialled her number, her phone was still off.

I sent her a text message.

There was a skylight above my bed. I looked at the sky, shrouded with clouds. On clear nights I could gaze at the moonlight and stars from my bed.

For an instant I closed my eyes that were aching from three days of awaiting sleep.

The key to my sleep house was broken. It was uncertain when its door would open and when it would close.

Shortly afterwards I half opened my eyes again.

When I looked at the clock on the wall I realized I had been asleep for exactly twelve hours.

The whole night seemed to have flashed by in an instant.

I shot out of bed.

I couldn't remember where I had left my phone.

It had fallen under the bed.

There were several messages. None of them from anyone I was expecting to hear from.

It was almost dawn.

I called Feruzeh again. Unavailable.

I hadn't eaten since the previous day.

I realized I was hungry.

I put on the kettle to make tea.

I spread butter and jam on stale bread for breakfast.

I watched the news on television.

If I had known anything about the news of the conflict that had been raging for several days in Mogadishu, the capital of Somalia, or the events that had taken place during the presidential election in Turkey, or the photograph of an Iraqi man tortured to death by British soldiers two days earlier, it would have made me anxious.

I felt as detached from this world as the Iraqi man tortured to death.

I took two painkillers.

The last news item I heard before I went out was that there had been an earthquake in Kent.

I went to the interpreting agency as soon as it opened. I borrowed some money from a Turkish friend and a Farsi-English dictionary from an Iranian interpreter.

They said I looked tired and complained that there was less and less work. We arranged to go to the cinema the following week.

It wasn't raining today.

As I was walking through the underpass beside the shopping centre I noticed the half-finished graffiti. The graffiti that the teenagers had climbed on each other's shoulders to paint on the high wall last week was incomplete. They had written, "The art of poetry is" but hadn't managed to finish it off. The last two letters were very faint, they must have run out of paint.

The art of poetry. Many years earlier a group of us had met in a *gecekondu* shack. One of us had said, "According to the laws of war a revolutionary's life is short." What could we squeeze into a short life? Everyone shared their dream. My dream was to publish a book of poetry and for my innocent gaze, captured in a photo, to be emblazoned on the commemorative posters my comrades would put up after I was gone, like Lorca who died in the war. But so far I hadn't done a very good job, either of turning my poems into a book, or of dying.

I walked to The Western Front antique shop where Feruzeh worked.

I needed to talk to Stella and get Azita's telephone number from her.

The antique shop was still closed.

I went into the café next door.

I had a cup of coffee and flicked through the tabloids on the table.

Towards midday Stella was still nowhere to be seen.

I asked the café staff. They said the antique shop had been closed yesterday too.

As I racked my brains for a plan I realized that everyone who had come into my life in this small city last week had suddenly disappeared.

I scribbled a short note on a scrap of paper and posted it through the antique shop's letterbox.

I walked all the way down the street, past the swimming pool and the big park.

I wandered around the market in the city centre.

I examined the food stalls, admired the brightly coloured jewellery, browsed through second-hand · books. I carefully inspected each stallholder's face.

My mind was on the telephone in my hand. Feruzeh could call at any moment.

I headed to the riverbank and mingled with the crowd sprawled out on the grass in Jesus Green Park.

I spent the afternoon strolling among the people in the park. Everyone having barbecues, playing volleyball, kissing, laughing, sunbathing and reading was happy.

I bumped into people I knew, but none of them were who I needed to see.

I sat under a Judas tree and lifted my head to look at the pink blossoms.

If I were to sleep here embracing the sunshine the world would go on for all eternity.

Perhaps I would hear Feruzeh's voice when I woke up. We would talk about our hopes, not our sins. We would gaze at the slight tilt of each other's necks, our slender fingers and the Judas blossoms.

My phone rang. I jumped to answer it.

It was a friend.

My weak heart became a little weaker.

I wandered along the riverbank, with no idea what to do. I turned back and watched the rowing boats.

I went to Feruzeh's house.

The curtains were still drawn.

I rang the bell. I pounded on the door.

I sat with my back against the wall I had propped my bike against the previous day.

I closed my eyes and leaned my head back. The sun flowed from my forehead towards my neck, like hot water.

I heard the voices of children walking past me.

A bicycle bell clanged. A girl walked past talking on her mobile phone.

Then a long silence followed.

I made a wish and opened my eyes but none of the people I wanted to see was anywhere near.

I slowly retraced the steps I had taken in my frozen state the previous day.

I felt sleepy.

Whenever I started sleeping again after a bout of sleepless nights my body took its revenge and my eyes closed even during the day.

My sight was now blurred and I felt dizzy.

From my dazed stagger people thought I was drunk.

A driver shouted "Bloody drunk!" when I crossed the road without looking at the traffic lights.

When I arrived at the Fort St George where Feruzeh and I had gone the first time we met the sun had set.

I sat outside.

I asked the two women sitting at the other end of the large table for a cigarette. I turned away so they wouldn't see what an inexperienced smoker I was. I covered my mouth as I choked on the smoke.

The huge park opposite the pub, with its orphaned trees, stretched endlessly before me. The grass under which plague victims had once been buried was now at peace. The lights in the houses on the other side of the road seemed as distant as the stars behind a mountain.

I wanted to shout like a drunk.

"Have a nice evening," I said and got up.

I examined every bicycle I saw on the off chance that it might be mine.

I bought a few groceries from the corner shop.

By the time I got home I was exhausted.

I sliced open half a loaf of bread and put cheese and tomatoes in it. I ate.

I drank lime blossom tea.

The television was still talking about the Iraqi man tortured to death by British soldiers.

The next story was about the earthquake.

I switched off the television and the light and got into bed.

I had no idea if the door of my sleep house was open. The fate of my nights depended on a broken key.

I thought about my book fortune poem of last week.

I remembered the lines that Feruzeh had translated from Farsi for me: "Let's believe in the beginning of the cold season."

Time passed.

I tossed and turned in bed, but in vain.

I realized I had been caught up in a maelstrom by continuously repeating the words about the beginning of the cold season.

I opened my eyes.

I picked up the Farsi-English dictionary on my bedside table.

I didn't need to get up and put on the light. The moonlight streaming through the skylight was enough.

Lit by the moon, I flicked through the pages of the dictionary.

I felt like Bach aged nine.

Bach had lost both his parents in his childhood and lived with his older brother, who gave him music lessons. His brother was wary of certain manuscripts, locking them away in a cupboard. At night, Bach waited until everyone was asleep then crept out of bed. He would squeeze his skinny hand through the bars of the cupboard and take the manuscripts, stay up all night reading them by moonlight and copy them onto separate sheets.

The dictionary in my hand was as precious as Bach's moonlight manuscripts.

I was searching for the Farsi equivalent of the words that touched Feruzeh's tongue and breath. I wanted to see the words that believed in the beginning of the cold season.

"Iman beyaverim be agazê faslê serd."

11
DENIZ

The Land of Mirrors

When I was little I was afraid of becoming one of those disloyal adults who desert their village. People who took off and left without another look back were traitors to their childhood. The villagers said it was fate's doing and resigned themselves to it. I was curious to know what my Uncle Hatip's fate was, and why, whatever the season, he always carried unfamiliar sorrow around with him on his radio. As I listened to the voices on the radio I used to think I was entering another world inside a mirror. In one of my mother's stories a man who entered another world escaped 1,001 near-deaths at the hands of djinns and *huts*, then returned. I sometimes feared that I wouldn't be able to return. Then, when I ventured out into the village in my entranced state, I would tell the children gathered impatiently around me the stories I had heard on the radio. I was a traveller come from far-off lands, an enigmatic stranger whom no one knew. The children who listened to me vowed with the determination of world-weary orphans that one day they would all depart for distant lands together. We were all blossoms from the same branch, I too vowed with them.

It was then that I started to retain every word I heard and to tell others the stories I listened to. But the children who listened to me breathlessly didn't know what patience was.

Man: "I will never put the feelings in my heart into words madam."

Woman: "Why not?"

Man: "Talking of what cannot be will hurt us both."

Woman: "Surely we can find a way."

Man: "You wouldn't speak that way if you knew what I was going to say."

The voices of the crowd, the rumble of an engine.

Woman: "The train is about to leave."

("What's a train?"/"How should I know, I heard it on the radio."/"You don't understand Turkish properly son, she must have said something else."/"I understood everything Madam said perfectly."/"What's 'Madam'?"/"The woman's name.")

Man: "I remember a scene like this in a novel."

Woman: "What happens?"

Man: "A young man is in love with a woman. Their love is hopeless. Yet the man tells the woman what his mind fears but his heart desires."

Woman: "What does the woman do?"

Man: "That doesn't matter, what matters is the end."

Woman: "What happens at the end?"

Man: "The woman commits suicide."

Woman: "That means she loves him."

The sound of a train.
("A train must be like a big bus."/"Let him get on with the story.")

Man: "If everyone who loves dies I want to spare you that
        fate."

Woman: "And the only way of doing that is by remaining
        silent?"

Man: "What my mind fears but my heart desires is …"

Woman: "Be quiet and kiss me."

Silence.

Woman: "I've waited so long for this moment. Kiss me again."

Silence.
*("Is he kissing her now?"/"Yeah."/"Make the silence last
a bit longer."/"Okay.")*
The silence continues.
The sound of a gunshot.
The crowd starts screaming.
Another gunshot.

Woman: "Ah, our love was even more short lived than the love
        in that novel."

Man: "Hold my hand madam, so we can die together."

*A whistle blows, gradually the sound of the train becomes
fainter.*
*("Shall we go and play the silence game with the
girls?"/"Come on then.")*

While I was telling stories all the children and I would enter
a mirror, then we had no choice but to come back. It was a
time when all the children tried to emulate a radio hero called
Deniz, we all lived in hope of meeting him inside the mirror.
Our hearts raced, we could barely breathe. We would hear Deniz

clapping his hands in the red breeze, and set off in pursuit of undiscovered shadows. When talking about Deniz, the adults would sometimes miss prayers, women's voices would break with grief, men would smoke one cigarette after another. Inside the mirror we would silently follow his tracks.

I was a puny child, my wildest dream was to be Deniz for just one day. We thought he was a sailor and used to honour the fastest swimmer in the stream with the name Deniz. I swam for all I was worth but always ran out of breath. While sleeping with my mother, father and four brothers and sisters in the one-room house inherited from Kewê, I would dream of swimming better the next day, occasionally screaming as I threw off the quilt that weighed down on my sleep. My mother would wake up, stroke my sweat-covered neck and kiss my hair. "Go to sleep Brani Tawo, go to sleep," she would say softly. I used to think she was saying "Deniz". Much as it pained me to lose the competition to be Deniz, I didn't know what unhappiness was. Everyone in the village was happy in their own way; unhappiness penetrated only the souls of those tied to cities. Pain and sorrow were something else, we were familiar with those. Although Deniz was a rebel we still insisted on thinking he was a sailor. While the whole world searched for him we didn't tell a soul that actually he lived inside the mirror.

One day some soldiers and men in suits came to the village. Uncle Hatip, my mother and I were listening to the radio. As had been the custom in those parts since the ancient tribal era, a wooden rafter placed in the centre of each room supported the roof of the houses. Homes with no centre rafter were considered poor, even if they were whitewashed with lime. In the same place as Kewê had sat thirty years previously, my mother was now leaning against the rafter, observing the world outside the open door. An armed man walked past the door. "Who's that?" I said.

My uncle replied, "A gendarme."

Then a man in a felt hat walked past. "Who's that?" I asked.

My uncle replied, "The tax inspector."

On the radio several people were talking at once. "Who are they?" I asked.

"The people in Ankara," said my uncle. The voices on the radio died down, my mother and uncle grew silent.

"And who are we?" I asked. They both looked at me.

That day, as the radio announced that Deniz and his friends had been executed, my ears rang and for the first time ever during my childhood I thought I hadn't heard the radio right. "The state killed him," they said.

"Who's 'the state'?" I asked. Whenever I asked that question the earth shook and the heavens thundered. Like every child destined to fail "state" in school, I realized that I had to hide Deniz in mirrors that no one knew about for the rest of my life. As the poet said:

The night that Deniz returned from afar,
A girl was combing her tresses before a dark mirror.
Outside were the horses' breath, radio stations and
The scent of freshly cut straw.
The locks had grown old, the doors aged.
The alarm bells,
The alarm bells insisted,
On ringing to announce the blight in every heart.
No one got up, no one ran to the window.
Then the bleary eyed children set out with Deniz,
One morning at daybreak to the land of mirrors.
And like trees abandoned in the cold,
The frost thrashed our hearts,
Thrashed our hearts.

I never saw Uncle Hatip again. He gave his carpet bag to my mother and left the village. I heard his story years later from my mother, when I was lying wounded in bed.

As a young man Uncle Hatip worked as a shepherd in the villages on the other side of Mangal Mountain. When, three months after his wedding he accidentally called his wife "Zahide" she felt as though he had stabbed her heart. "Who is this Zahide?" she screamed, her shrieks reverberating throughout the neighbourhood. It was a miracle she didn't miscarry the child she was pregnant with. Uncle Hatip's mind went blank; he had no idea where he had got the name Zahide. There were no Zahides, either in his own family, or in this village where he was a shepherd.

The following day, when he was driving his flock out to pasture, he forgot his food bundle at home. He went hungry all day and for that reason brought the flock back to the village a little earlier than usual. If he had not returned home early that day he would have met a caravan of gypsies. When he discovered that the most beautiful girl in the caravan was called Zahide, he would have fallen in love on the spot, like prisoners sentenced to death who lack the strength to struggle against fate. Uncle Hatip would have abandoned his wife and home to run away with the gypsy caravan, roamed distant villages and been knifed to death seven years later in a brawl that started over Zahide. But because he returned from pasture early that day, none of it happened.

Uncle Hatip discovered the unwritten part of his fate when he went to the next village to buy a new gun. The gypsy caravan was in the next village; an elderly, blind gypsy related it all and described my uncle when she mentioned "a shepherd who will come to buy a gun" whilst telling a fortune. When the gypsy asked, "Is unfulfilled destiny better or worse?" everyone listening to her chorused "Worse." The blind gypsy contented herself with taking a drag from her cigarette and scorning the villagers with her ancient cackle.

Uncle Hatip shuddered, first to discover there was a Zahide amongst the gypsies, and again, when he learned his other fate. On his way home in the light of the full moon he resolved to tell his wife everything, but she wasn't there. The neighbours said, "She left, with her pregnant belly." Everyone knew what it was to love, but being loved was in the hands of fate. That night, as he fired bullets at the full moon, Uncle Hatip realized that it was only now that he was about to embark on his real destiny.

He searched high and low in the villages on the plain and the distant valleys, agonizing night and day over whether his child was a girl or a boy. As the years passed he thought his daughter must be tall like her mother who had abandoned him or, in case he had had a son, he described a youth who looked like himself to everyone he met. "Look at my face carefully," he would announce in village squares. "Everyone is a lake, until the full moon shines on his face. I am seeking my full moon." Sometimes he didn't know exactly what he was pursuing; he would join gypsy caravans that he met on his travels and spend seasons at a time with them, crossing hills and dales. He described no one to the gypsies, he did not say, "Look at my face," he only asked after Zahide. But while life aged, like a tree in the autumn winds, my uncle did not manage to find Zahide either. He smoked tobacco constantly, and the tobacco smoke cauterized his heart. At a time when he was as much in need of new hope as a child who can't sleep he bumped into Tatar the photographer in one of the coffeehouses in Haymana. While looking at the photographs Tatar had taken in the villages, he realized that his life had crashed to the ground and shattered, like a picture engraved on glass. Their fates were as similar as the leaves on a tree; Tatar and my uncle were roaming the villages on the plain for the same reason.

I remember the sorrow on my uncle's face the last time he came to the village when I was still a child. Life was as sacred as a holy book whose every page had been turned and finished but the contents of which remained unknown. My uncle wandered amongst those pages, lamenting and growing pale. Inside the carpet bag he gave my mother on the last day, when he was leaving, there were some old photographs and a camera. My mother had no idea when Tatar the photographer gave the camera to my uncle, but she remembered the camera clearly. While Tatar was taking photographs of her and Kewê during my mother's childhood she had examined the camera carefully and realized that a destiny was being created inside it, and that from that day a new garden of life would unravel before her.

12
STELLA

The White Shirt

I got out of bed.
I checked my phone to see if I had received any calls.
I showered.
I had breakfast in front of the television.
It was a beautiful day.
Outside the bright light beckoned.

I picked out my white shirt from the clean laundry basket and ironed it. I was wearing it on the day I met Feruzeh.

On my way out I didn't look at the photograph on the wall.

I went down to the river.

I walked beside the joggers and the people rowing on the river.

I walked through crowded streets and arrived at the graveyard where Wittgenstein lay.

I saw the old man from last week at the window of the house on the street leading to the cemetery. He was watching the outside world. I smiled and waved at him.

I looked at my phone, as though it would ring that very minute.

I ambled in slow motion amongst the rustling leaves.

I couldn't see the gravediggers. I wondered whether they worked in the rain and had sunny days off.

I stopped beside several gravestones, trying to guess their inhabitants' stories.

The shadows of the trees shading the graves contained clues of the lives of the dead, like the lines on the palm of a hand.

I went behind the church.

I reached Wittgenstein's grave. The people who had remembered the anniversary of his death had placed bouquets of flowers by the gravestone.

I sat on the dry earth.

Following Anatolian tradition, I cleared some dried leaves from the grave and sprinkled water from my bottle over it.

Anyone who saw me would realize I intended to spend the whole day there.

The sun was scorching my forehead.

I took a poetry book out of my bag and opened a page at random.

When I was a child I remember a crying man reading poetry on the radio one day. I realized then that one shouldn't cry when reading poetry.

Children received their share of the village harvest too. Everyone who harvested crops gave the children two handfuls each of wheat, which we exchanged for biscuits and *lokum* from the pedlar. I refused the wheat of the children who offered it to me in return for reading them poetry. Poetry, which at that time was as sacred as prayer, could not be measured with wheat. But I did sometimes accept the *lokum* they offered me after I had read the poetry.

When I was a child, touching earth and wheat made me feel alive. Our village became rooted in time, along with the earth and the wheat. Contrary to what they believed in cities, a person's history did not begin with their oldest family member.

I finished the poem and put the book back in my bag.

I looked around.

I was alone with several hundred gravestones.

I lay down beside Wittgenstein's grave. The same soil was beneath us and the same sky above us.

I closed my eyes.

I imagined there was a gravestone above me. A large, grey, flat gravestone.

I started singing a folk-song, so loud the last cadaver by the furthest wall could have heard.

Birds flew away. Branches rustled.

The sound of music came from the other side of the wall.

A violin was playing.

I stopped to listen. The violin stopped too.

I opened my eyes.

I waited a while.

I began the song again.

The violin accompanied my voice.

We continued in unison.

It was the same folk-song Kewê had heard the labourers sing in the field and had then sung to my mother forty years later. Whenever I sang that song I imagined myself beneath that night's red breeze. I remained true to the memory of that starry night when Kewê was in love.

The day I had told Feruzeh Kewê's story she had asked me to sing the song to her. Blushing like a bashful child I had said, "It's not the right time."

Here I was now, sharing the song I had never sung in front of anyone with the dead.

The sun warmed my face and my voice.

It had been years since I'd stretched out on the ground like this. My skin was sprouting roots down into the soil.

My song ended.

The violin fell silent.

The birds returned, the branches' shadows quivered.

I should get up, take some bread from my bag and scatter the crumbs over the grave. I had read that in a Dostoevsky novel. When the birds came to eat the bread the dead would hear them singing.

My phone rang. I answered without looking to see who it was.

It was a friend inviting me to a picnic by the river.

I should have kept my phone switched off while I was there. Being with the dead was as sacred as entering the temple of sleep. But for the past few days I had kept my phone on even while I was sleeping.

I sat up. I looked at Wittgenstein's grave. The red roses by the gravestone shone in the sunlight.

A sparrow landed beside the roses and hopped a couple of paces. My phone rang again. The sparrow flapped its wings and flew away.

I didn't recognize the number. A woman said she was calling from the Western Front antique shop. She was a friend of Stella's, and had seen my note when she had passed by the shop to pick up a few things.

"Stella's in hospital," she said.

I took the slices of bread out of my bag. I broke them into small pieces and scattered them over Wittgenstein's grave.

I went to the bus stop.

A thousand and one thoughts flashed through my mind on the way to Addenbrooke's Hospital. I bought a bunch of flowers at the hospital entrance.

I went up to the third floor and found Stella's ward.

The nurse pointed out the bed by the window. I opened the curtain a crack.

Stella was asleep.

I sat down on the chair beside her.

I put the flowers down on the bedside table.

The wires on Stella's chest were connected to a screen.

I examined the screen. Although I didn't understand them I decided that the numbers and readings were all what they should be.

I contemplated the lines on her face.

Her pale skin was now a little paler, her hair looked thinner.

I bent down and listened to her breathing. Her breath was deep, warm and old.

Feruzeh had told me that Stella had a son who lived abroad. I wondered if he knew.

Slowly, Stella half opened her eyes. She paused.

"Hello young man," she said.

"Hello dear lady," I replied.

She tried to sit up.

I raised the headboard to a vertical position and plumped up her pillows.

"What time is it?" she asked.

I told her.

"Would you like some water?" I said.

"Yes please."

One night her chest had felt tight. She had called the emergency services and the ambulance had reached her in time.

"What do the doctors say?"

"I'm over the age limit, but they say I'm going to get better."

"How long are you going to be in here?"

"Who knows."

"Don't rush to leave," I said.

She smiled.

"These past few days I've been thinking about my first encounter with death …"

"Where was that?"

"On the deck of a ship."

"Was it a very long time ago?"

"I was a teenager during the Second World War. They drafted me into a nursing unit One day they told us we were going abroad. We boarded a ship one stormy night and it wasn't long before the Germans attacked us and our ship sank. They only managed to pull four of us out of the waves alive. I was like a skinny boy with short hair. We were covered in petrol. They undressed us on the deck and hosed us down. That night I thought I would die in the war like my grandfather. My grandfather was one of those million soldiers who died in the Battle of the Somme in the previous war."

She stopped.

"Would you like some water?" I said.

"I just need to get my breath," she said.

She waited.

"When he saw I was a woman the German officer said, 'What's this little girl doing on this ship?' He separated me from the others and sent me back to England. The feeling of death soon went away, but it came back again at the end of the war. The boy I loved never returned; he hasn't even got a grave ..."

Without asking I passed her a glass of water.

She took a sip.

"I remember that rainy, windy night on that ship's deck like it was yesterday," she said.

"It sounds like a scene from a war movie," I said.

"War movies take me right back to that time," she replied. "You're lucky, you didn't have to go to war like us."

I said nothing. I paused.

I took the glass out of her hand.

"Do you need anything?" I said.

"That's very kind of you. A friend came this morning; I asked her to bring me a few things."

"Does your son know you're in hospital?" I asked.

"No. There's no point in worrying him."

"I'm sure he would want to come if he knew you were ill," I said.

"He lives in Canada. He's got a very demanding job."

"Maybe he could just come for a day …"

"He was only here last month."

I didn't think of the loneliness of sons living in far-off countries, but of the mothers they left all alone.

My mother didn't tell me everything when I telephoned either. I listened to what she said, but tried to gauge what she wasn't telling me.

"Did you come alone?" asked Stella.

She didn't know about Feruzeh.

I updated her.

"So Feruzeh went to Iran on the day I came into hospital; that would explain why her phone's switched off. I asked the nurses to phone her yesterday," she said.

"I thought you'd know."

"Feruzeh must have phoned the antique shop and the house before she went," she said thoughtfully. "I don't have a mobile phone."

I remembered that mobile phones had to be switched off in hospitals.

I hesitated for a moment.

I took my phone out of my pocket. I pressed the off key. I didn't take my eyes off the screen until the light went off.

"Have you got Feruzeh's mother's mobile number?" I asked.

"I've only got their landline," she replied.

"They're not at home," I said.

The visitors of the patient on the other side of the curtain were talking about their summer holidays. We listened to them for a while.

Stella asked me the time.

I told her.

"I've found out the make of the camera you're looking for," she said.

"Really?"

She smiled.

"Olympus Six," she said.

"Is it a well-known camera?" I asked.

"Yes. It came out during the Second World War," she said. "The moment I saw it in the photo it looked familiar."

"Do you think we'll be able to find it?"

"It'll be easier than finding Einstein's camera. I've asked a friend of mine in London to look for it."

"Thank you."

"Is it very important to you?"

"I'm going to give it to my mother."

"Feruzeh has told me some of your mother's and uncle's stories."

"Actually he was my mother's uncle. We used to call him uncle too."

"If you'd stayed in the village you would have ended up looking like your uncle in that sun."

"That's what my mother says," I said.

Stella stopped, as though tired. She took a deep breath.

"Are you all right? Shall I call the nurse?" I said.

"I'm always like this. Sometimes I need to take a deep breath."

"Would you like some water?" I said.

"No, thank you," she said.

She paused a moment.

"You were talking about your uncle ..." she said.

"When I was a child I used to ask 'where did I come from?' My mother and the neighbours, the 'aunties', would laugh. I didn't believe their answers. Sometimes I used to wake up in the middle of the night and listen to the silence. I used to think I disappeared in the darkness. I was as curious about how I had come into the world as I was about death."

"Do you know the answer now?" asked Stella.

The lines in her face got deeper when she smiled.

"My Uncle Hatip left his camera with my mother the last time he came to the village. I used to think that if I could find out how that machine made people I would discover the answer to the question about myself too. One day when there was no one at home I took the camera out from its hiding place amongst all the colourful headscarves in the chest. I went to the stream bed. I was so excited my heart was about to split in two. I smashed the machine open with a stone. There was nothing inside except screws and small pieces of metal. The question in my heart had become too oppressive for my feeble mind to bear. I cried hysterically."

I paused for a moment.

I breathed heavily, like an old man, then continued.

"I picked up the broken pieces from amongst the weeds. I took them home and put them back in the chest. My mother didn't find out for months. One rainy day we heard that my uncle had died. My mother wailed in lament. She took my uncle's things out of the chest. She stopped dead when she saw the camera smashed to pieces amongst the colourful headscarves. She held her breath and I burst into tears and flung my arms around her. Through her tears my mother kissed my hair and never brought it up again."

I fell silent.

Stella looked at me with maternal tenderness.

"Feruzeh and I came up with all sorts of theories about your camera," she said.

"What sort of theories?" I said.

"The first day you came we talked about why you might be looking for that camera. But all our guesses were wrong."

"You should have asked me."

"Haven't you told Feruzeh yet?"

"No."

"You can tell her when she gets back."

"When she gets back ..."

"Don't worry, she'll be back," she said.

"I hope so ..." I said.

Her face broke into a smile that filled me with hope.

She looked out of half-closed eyes.

"She must have made up with her sister after this," she said.

"Weren't they talking?" I asked.

"Didn't you know?" she said.

"No," I replied.

She paused. She closed her eyes.

The visitors of the patient in the next bed were complaining about how awful last year's holiday had been.

Stella opened her eyes and looked at me.

"That white shirt suits you," she said.

"I like wearing white in spring," I said.

I didn't tell her I had gone to the cemetery.

We paused for a moment.

"Feruzeh was going to tell you. Do you think I should tell you instead?"

"I think you have to," I said.

"I've already let the cat out of the bag. I can't leave you hanging like this."

"No, you can't," I said.

She asked for some water.

I filled her glass from the jug.

She took just two sips to wet her lips.

"What's the time?" she asked.

I told her.

Then, very slowly, she spoke.

"Feruzeh met an Iranian. He was a tall young man, I don't remember his name, he had big black eyes like yours. They were planning to get married and go back to Iran. But for some reason unknown to any of us the young Iranian went back to Iran alone. Roya was studying in London at that time."

"Roya?"

"Feruzeh's twin."

"I didn't know her name."

"Everyone thought Roya was in London, but one day Feruzeh got a letter from her from Iran. It said she was in love with the Iranian, that she had tried to resist it, that she had even taken an overdose, but her flatmates had found her and rushed her to hospital. She had no more strength left after that, either to resist or to die. She spoke to the Iranian and left with him."

Stella was whispering so the people on the other side of the curtain wouldn't hear.

"Roya blamed Feruzeh. She said the young Iranian had been her friend, that she had been attracted to him. She introduced Feruzeh to him but never imagined they would get together. Then she kept quiet and for a long time she just accepted the situation."

My breath slowed down until I thought it would stop.

I took my water bottle out of my bag.

I took a sip.

I waited.

I took another sip.

Stella took up where she had left off: "Feruzeh said that wasn't true, that she didn't know Roya loved him."

I dropped the bottle.

The curtains opened.

"Is everything all right?" asked the nurse.

I picked up the plastic bottle from the floor.

"It's nothing, I just dropped this," I said.

"Everything's fine," added Stella.

The nurse went out, smiling.

"What's more dangerous: a woman whose pride has been injured or a wounded tiger?" asked Stella.

"I know that one," I said.

"Feruzeh and Roya were both hurt, and they hurt each other."

I needed to get out of there and go back to Wittgenstein's grave.

There I would meet other people dressed in white.

Stella asked me to write my name on a piece of paper.

"I'm going to try and pronounce your name," she said.

I wrote it down and gave it to her.

She read it, spelling out the sounds.

"Bre-ni Te-wo."

I said it, and she repeated.

"Bra-ni Ta-wo ..." Her gaze was like a glittering mirror.

She held out her hand and touched my fingers.

I bowed my head to avoid her eyes.

13
TATAR THE PHOTOGRAPHER

War Spoils

The war had not yet started. During the old man Os' first and only visit to Ankara in search of a treasure he was hunting, he had his photograph taken with two friends. He posed before the camera still as a corpse, wondering what was inside it, then set out on his return journey. His two friends were supposed to collect the photograph but the following day the photographer told them the film had been ruined and that he had to redo the photos. "Our third friend isn't here," they said.

"Don't worry," said the photographer, "I'll take care of everything." He stopped a passer-by who had a beard like the old man Os'. He put a jacket on him, sat him down and handed him a long string of prayer beads.

When the old man Os saw the photograph that his friends brought him a week later, he said, "It looks like me, but it's as though I'm not me." For several nights he couldn't sleep, he wandered around in the dark, he stopped praying. His soul had been snatched out of his chest, at every call to prayer he turned his head and stared at the photo hanging on the wall. Snow fell, flowers bloomed and the years flew by like a harvest wind. One summer day, seeing that a photographer had come to the village, the old man Os knocked on every door one by one. "Photographers try to imitate God by creating humans, but they leave them as soulless as dry soil," he said.

Tatar the photographer had been a photographer with his brother in Istanbul, and after the war he had set up in business on his own. His brother, who became known as the sergeant from Istanbul during the war, chose a different path by marrying Saadet and settling in Ankara. The soldiers who had returned from the war had left it in the hands of time to heal their invisible scars and ease the pain in their memories. The sergeant from Istanbul had laudable dreams, he loved his wife, he put bread on his table. He exerted himself, until the screaming and the corpses he had taken away as war spoils dragged him into the darkness.

The fate of some soldiers was to die in the war; those who happened to survive did not recover but tumbled headlong into life's pit of torment. The sergeant from Istanbul stumbled, became dazed, and eventually, like a rejected child, spent his nights in dens of iniquity. Heedless of his wife waiting at the window every night, he waved his knife menacingly at anyone who crossed his path in the dark. His fame spread as the number of corpses mounted, and his mind became more and more hazy. On one of those nights the sergeant from Istanbul entered the house of his old commander, meaning to claim his wife back. The commander ordered him out of there as though ordering him out of a shelter during the war, but he, believing it was enemy soldiers shouting at him, drew his gun and riddled everyone there with bullet holes.

The news didn't reach Istanbul until several days later. Tatar the photographer was sipping coffee in front of his shop one evening, chatting to his neighbour. There was no one at home waiting for him and one day passed pretty much like another. An acquaintance dropped by to say hello. "Do they call your brother the sergeant from Istanbul?" he asked, and told him what he had heard from a teacher from Ankara. Tatar the photographer

gave the key of the shop to his neighbour and set off without so much as stopping by his house.

At that time, the city of Ankara was the black and white version of colour cities. Everyone was like everyone else, a stranger stood out there immediately. Tatar the photographer searched for both Saadet, whom he knew was pregnant, and for his brother. He enquired at hospitals and police stations. He collected old newspapers and read about the murders his brother had committed. He went to Saadet's parents' graves and waited there for several nights. One day an old man who came to the grave told him what he had heard, which was that Saadet, left with no family, had heeded her father's words and gone to Haymana Plain and that she now lived in a village there. No one knew anything about the whereabouts of the sergeant from Istanbul; he might be spotted in any tavern or emerge from any dark street.

Tatar the photographer chatted to drunks and became the confidant of vagrants who were ready not to die but to kill. He tried to grasp how his brother, once a placid son of Istanbul, had turned into one of these men. One night he got wind of three vagabonds picking a fight with the sergeant from Istanbul in a downtown tavern. Tatar ran as fast his legs would carry him, and joined the crowd at the back of the tavern. His brother was standing alone a few feet away. The knife in his hand glinted in the light of the full moon, the blood of the three vagabonds lying at his feet flowed black and white into the soil.

Tatar wriggled free of the throng and pushed his way to the front. The crowd tensed and took a step back. The sergeant from Istanbul stared at the man before him like a peasant seeing a statue for the first time. He did not step forwards or backwards but took several steps to the side. Tatar held out his arms and the crowd retreated another step.

Fear on people's faces was the same in this city as anywhere else. The sergeant from Istanbul, who knew that, turned around and walked slowly away. He walked down the street and Tatar followed him. They roamed the back streets until daybreak, one in front, the other behind, pursued by a crowd. Patiently, they continued on their way without uttering a sound, as though they had embarked on a sacred voyage, until they found themselves before an enormous grey building. As the sky grew light behind the enormous grey building the sergeant from Istanbul stopped and waited, his head bowed. Tatar approached gently, embraced him and called him, "My brother." The vagabonds and vagrants stared wide-eyed, as though sobering up from the wine they had imbibed for so many years. They did not understand why the sergeant from Istanbul was embracing his older brother now. The two brothers remained locked in their embrace for some time. Then the sergeant from Istanbul suddenly thrust the knife he was holding into his brother's hand and plunged it into his own stomach. "I've killed all my enemies, the honour of killing me will go to none but my brother," he said. Like a child desperate to be held he cast his body into his brother's arms. As the poet said:

> He who forgets to count the days,
> Is wildly happy or sadly beckons death.
> A single raindrop can save him,
> Or a friend's hand may free him from life's somnolence.

"He killed the sergeant from Istanbul!" they cried. They led Tatar away from the spot where he was kneeling. In jail one day passed pretty much like another. As Tatar the photographer counted the years, he added his brother's blood to his own destiny. He wove kilims during the day and read books through the night. He learned Kurdish by listening to stories of bandits from prisoners that came from Haymana Plain. He memorized the names of the villages in the plain and the peaks stretching out into the distance. He knew that Saadet had gone to Haymana

Plain but couldn't find out which village she was in. Every day he studied the photographs the sergeant from Istanbul had had taken with his commander on the front and prepared himself to search for a woman who looked like the commander. The years did not remind him that he had aged and that the people he needed to find were growing further away.

When he got out of prison he didn't set foot in Istanbul, but wandered from one impoverished village of Haymana Plain to another taking photographs. A photograph seized a person's soul in its grip, no one could hide their true face from it. One drop contained a thousand teardrops, one smile a thousand meanings. Tatar the photographer sometimes imagined that someone would come and throw her arms around him declaring, "I'm the woman you're looking for." Then, remembering that the truth lay in photographs, he spread out the images he had taken on the floor every morning, searching for a child with his brother's gaze and a woman who looked like the commander. He roamed for many seasons, unaware that Saadet had had not one but two children and that since the grizzly bear's attack she had become known as the Claw-faced woman.

On one of the days when Tatar the photographer concealed his secret like a hidden treasure he came across Uncle Hatip in a Haymana coffeehouse. Tatar perceived that the patience in his voice was in fact weariness, and that he was running in breathless pursuit of a lost destiny. He ordered tea and offered him tobacco. When he learned that Uncle Hatip was looking for his wife and child he showed him the photographs in his bag. "The people you're looking for may be here," he said.

The two men's friendship began there on that day, but Tatar the photographer did not reveal his own secret to my uncle, he didn't tell him why he went from village to village taking photographs. Their paths separated and they followed the trail of their own stories. They met every season and chatted about the places, caravans and people they had left behind. They could not catch up with the pace of that horse called time. One day they mentioned their childhood and their relatives who were now dead. They talked of their memories. Tatar the photographer showed Uncle Hatip photographs of his family and said that his brother had died in the war. Uncle Hatip looked at the photographs one by one, pausing when he came to one in particular. He squinted. In the photograph the sergeant from Istanbul was standing, the hatless commander sitting on the ground. A red breeze was blowing. Uncle Hatip sipped his tea and took a drag from his cigarette. "This man looks like the Claw-faced woman," he said.

"Who does?" said Tatar.

"This commander."

14
O'HARA

The Art of Poetry

The phone rang.

It was a friend from London.

"You weren't at the rally yesterday …"

"I couldn't make it."

"Was it your insomnia again?"

"Yes."

"Have you heard about what's happened in Istanbul?"

"They called me last night. Some of our comrades have been arrested."

"I think we should bring the meeting forward, what do you say?"

"Good idea, let me know when you've set the date."

"Have you finished the article?"

"Nearly. I'm studying the files from Istanbul."

I put the phone on the floor.

I stayed in bed for another hour.

I tried to guess the weather by looking through the skylight.

I got up and switched on the television.

I called the interpreting agency and asked if they had any work for the following week.

I went out and breathed in the fresh air.

There were a couple of rowing boats on the river.

I strolled past whitewashed houses in silent streets.

Inside the underpass by the shopping centre the writing on the wall caught my eye. The teenagers had finished the "The Art of Poetry is" graffiti that they had abandoned halfway through when they ran out of paint. They had climbed up and written "The Art of Poetry is Dying".

I stood before the graffiti. The passers-by looked, not at the death of poetry, but at me.

I went to the city centre.

I listened to the buskers.

In the market I browsed among the brightly coloured dresses, the beaded jewellery and the fresh fruit.

I bought a coffee from the refreshments van and I sat beside the fountain in the market square.

A number of students from different countries were showing each other their purchases. An Indian T-shirt, an orange scarf and a leather bracelet passed from one hand to another.

I finished my coffee and resumed my perusal of the stalls.

I flicked through the second-hand books.

The man on the bread stall caught my eye. I asked him where he was from.

"Ireland ..." said a voice behind me.

I turned to look, and recognized the owner of the voice. He was the man with the black-framed glasses that I had met at Azita's birthday party.

"Hello O'Hara," I said.

He came and shook my hand.

"Hello Brani Tawo," he said.

"You remember my name," I said.

"Of course," he said. "Meet my father."

I greeted the elderly man on the stall.

"I thought he looked like you, that's why I asked where he was from."

"You thought he looked like me even though I have glasses?" asked O'Hara.

"Yes."

His father asked me where I was from, what I did and how long I had been here. He told me to try and bear life in England.

He pointed at the old man on the next stall. "This place would be all right if it wasn't for the damn English," he said.

"If it wasn't for us you'd all still be rotting in your villages," retorted the old stallholder.

"It's a damn good job we came to your cities, or your women would never have got to see any real men."

Both old men cackled with laughter.

"They're off again," said O'Hara.

"It looks like it could go on forever," I said.

A toddler ran past us with her small uncertain steps; her mother caught her.

O'Hara said, "I asked Feruzeh for your phone number."

"Really?"

"I was going to phone you this week."

"Have you seen Tina lately?" I asked.

"No, I've been at a conference in Paris, I got back this morning."

"A conference?"

"A philosophy conference."

"Aren't you a baker?"

"This is my dad's stall, I give him a hand occasionally."

I hesitated.

"Do you have Tina's telephone number?" I said.

"Yes. What's up?"

I told him what had happened last week. About Feruzeh going to Iran and Azita not being at home.

O'Hara called. He couldn't get through to Tina.

"Do you have a moment? Let's go for a walk," I said.

His father and the neighbour were still bickering with each other and laughing.

We each got a cup of coffee from the van.

We went down the side street by the church.

We sat on the wall of King's College in the street behind it.

"Feruzeh has told me about you and your political activities," I said.

"She's told me about you too," he said.

We laughed.

"She's taken it upon herself to act as the go-between for our organizations."

"Sometimes these things work by instinct."

An elderly couple came and stood in front of us. They looked at the plaque on the second floor of the house opposite.

"Our comrades are trying to organize a meeting with your people in London," I said.

"Do you have connections?" asked O'Hara.

"We did. They broke down when the peace talks between your organization and the British government got serious."

"Let me know if there's anything I can do to help," he said.

"I will, thank you."

O'Hara raised his coffee cup. "To better days," he said.

I also raised my coffee cup.

"To better days."

We looked at the passers-by.

"Feruzeh can travel to Iran. But Tina and Azita can't legally," he said.

"They must have taken a risk," I said.

"They can't go without a fake passport."

"They must have got one."

"No, they can't. Not without me."

"Were you going to get them a passport?"

"Yes, Tina knows that I can pull a few strings."

A few feet away a girl was playing the violin and another girl was dancing.

"Do you think she'll come back?" I asked.

"Who, Feruzeh?"

"Yes."

"Do *you* think she'll come back?"

"I don't know," I said.

"Two weeks ago you were at the re-enactment of the slave Olaudah's wedding ..."

"I met Feruzeh there ..."

"Tina couldn't make it because she had the flu, so Feruzeh used her invitation."

"Were you there?" I asked.

"I gave a speech."

"Was it you who gave the speech on destiny?"

"It was."

"You weren't wearing your glasses," I said.

"I had my contact lenses in," he said.

"You said that although he was a slave abducted from Africa Olaudah managed to forge his own destiny."

"He couldn't go back to Africa but he created his own Africa."

"How can I create Africa without Feruzeh," I said.

"Isn't Feruzeh your Africa?"

I nodded.

"Either you wait for your Africa to come to you, or you go off in search of your own Africa," he said.

"Then I'll go after her," I said.

"To Iran."

"Yes, but ..."

I hesitated.

I took a sip of my coffee.

O'Hara looked at me.

"But ...?" he repeated.

"I need a passport," I said.

A young couple asked me to take a photograph of them. They posed arm in arm in front of the house opposite.

"You want me to sort you out with a passport," said O'Hara.

"If possible," I said.

"It's possible but it will take time," he said.

"How long?"

"A few weeks," he said.

"I couldn't ask my own friends to help me with something so personal," I said.

"I understand," he said.

"Thank you so much," I said. "For Africa."

He laughed.

He raised his coffee cup.

"For all the Africas," he said.

"For all the Africas."

The street had become crowded and the noise drowned out the tunes of the girl playing the violin.

"We think you and Feruzeh make a good couple."

"Who does?"

"Tina, Azita and me."

"Did Azita say that?"

"Not in so many words. But I know the way Iranian women's minds work."

"Iranian women's? Is their character so uniform?"

"All right then, the women in this family. Is that better?"

"Will you teach me too?"

"What?"

"Teach me how you understand them."

"You can't teach it," he said. "You can only learn by being with them."

He looked at me and smiled.

O'Hara and I agreed not to speak by phone. I would contact him by going to the bread stall and giving his father a photo of myself.

We said our goodbyes and I set off for home.

As I was walking through the underpass I saw a woman standing before the sign announcing: "The Art of Poetry is Dying". She had a little girl with her and they were looking at the graffiti.

When I arrived home my hands were shaking.

I was exhausted, even though I hadn't done anything.

I figured a bath would do me good.

I filled the bathtub and lay in the hot water with my eyes shut. I daydreamed that I was back at home with my family. I wandered through the fields. I sat down in a pavement coffeehouse.

Whenever I was suddenly overcome with exhaustion I felt dizzy and my muscles grew weak.

My hands were still shaking when I got out of the bath.

I hadn't felt faint for months but I could feel that I was about to pass out.

I lay on the bed.

I drifted into a dream. I watched the crowd around me and I saw soldiers running towards me. The sun suddenly vanished, time became eternal. The soldiers roared as they beat me. I heard the sound the bones in my face made as they broke. My whole body was soaked in blood. My eyes met those of a small girl. She held out her hand to help me. I smiled. She smiled back. I turned and looked behind me. I saw a large field of crops. My blood flowed heavier. The ears of wheat turned red. I heard a voice say, "Okay, he's dead." My nostrils filled with the smell of blood. The whole world turned black. In the distance a woman sang the same song over and over again and a telephone rang insistently.

The wide-winged bird of time hung suspended in the void.

Slowly I opened my eyes.

I looked at my watch. It had been three hours since I had gone to bed.

This was the first time I had dreamt in a long time. Fainting was good for my mental exhaustion.

The telephone rang again.

The woman on the other end said, "Brani Tawo."

I would have known that voice in a thousand.

"Azita," I said.

"Have I called at a bad time? You're out of breath …"

"No, no, no …"

My neck, my back, my stomach were all soaked in sweat.

I took a deep breath.

Azita was at Tina's house. They had gone to London after she had seen Feruzeh off. They had received O'Hara's message late because she had gone to the hospital for a check-up.

I told her I had left a note at their house, that I had called our common acquaintances, that Stella had had a heart attack and that I had seen O'Hara at the market.

"Everything happened so quickly, we didn't think to ask Feruzeh for your telephone number," she said.

"I can't get through to Feruzeh," I said.

"Her phone doesn't work abroad. She only realized after she got there," she said.

"Have you been in touch?"

"She's phoned once," she said.

"Do you have a number where I can call her?"

"Unfortunately not," she said.

"How is Roya, is she okay?"

"She's in hospital," she said.

I could feel her voice breaking.

"She recovered last time, and she'll recover this time too," I said.

"There was I fearing I would die far away from Iran, and now my daughter is there fighting death."

I didn't tell Azita I was going to Iran. There was still time.

"Have you told any book fortunes recently?" I asked.

She remained silent.

After a pause she said, "No I haven't. After they imprisoned my husband I was afraid of telling book fortunes; I thought I would never feel fear like that again."

"Try the book I gave you for your birthday," I said.

"I'm glad you reminded me; I want to thank you again for your present."

"You're welcome. Do you like it?"

"I don't just like it, I'm overwhelmed."

"Why?"

"I can see you've gone to great pains to decorate it. You've put a different flower on each page."

"It's the first poetry book I bought in England. I dried the small flowers I picked from parks and stuck them on the edge of each page."

"I'm not sure I'm the person who should have this book," she said.

"I just obeyed the voice inside me," I said. "It doesn't matter which page you open when you're telling a fortune, with that book you will always come across a flower."

We both paused.

We listened to the humming of the telephone.

"Where did you get that song?" she asked.

"Which song?" I said.

" 'Hejrat'. I can hear it from my end of the phone," she said.

I stopped for a moment. I didn't remember when I had put the CD player on. "Feruzeh gave it to me," I said.

"Brani Tawo …"

"Yes …"

"You shouldn't listen to melancholy songs," she said.

"Okay, I won't," I said.

I bowed my head, the phone still in my hand.

"Are you patient?" she asked.

"If I know how things will turn out, then I'm patient. But uncertainty weighs heavier than time," I said.

"Brani Tawo …"

My heart relaxed as Azita pronounced my name.

"Do you realize how much you've changed Feruzeh?" she said.

"No," I said.

"After her sister left, Feruzeh didn't touch her book of secrets again. She lost faith in poetry. But two weeks ago she met you, and she took her book with the rose design out of the cupboard again and started carrying it around with her every day."

I raised my head and gazed up at the sky through the skylight. The stars were shining.

15
HACO

People are People's Refuge

On the day that Tatar the photographer came to the village the people who had gathered in Kewê and Haco's house left in the middle of the night. Some went off in search of the Claw-faced woman's daughters while others went to the south peak as soon as they heard that my father had been struck by lightning. All the houses were suddenly deserted; no one but young girls, children and the elderly remained in the village.

Having seen his guests to the door, Haco rolled a cigarette and sat down in front of the door. Once again, a solitary bird that had perched on the apple tree was chirping in the darkness. The spring water flowed cheerfully, like a child with boundless energy. Once she had spread out the beds Kewê went to the door. Seeing Haco slumped on the ground she panicked, and called out to my ten-year-old mother. They carried Haco to bed and sprinkled water on his face. He opened his eyes and looked at Kewê. "I wanted to die after you," he said, "so you wouldn't be left alone all over again."

Haco, who had been an old man when he had arrived in the village, had started to work as an imam, and one day he had asked Kewê if she would accept him as her husband. Kewê was sitting under the apple tree. She had looked at Haco's long white hair, then broken off a piece of the apple in her hand and held it out to him. Haco had told her then about his past.

"My father and I used to travel from village to village sharpening knives; we had a herd of horses that went everywhere with us. Whatever a bird is to a birdman, or his beloved to a man in love, that's how much my father adored his black horses. He would turn the blunt knives on the grinding stone and treat everyone who gathered around him to horse stories. When he touched my hair it was as though his hand was stroking a horse's mane. Before he died he told me to set the horses free in the steppe. I married in the village where my father died and started working as an imam and prepared to be a loving father. But I never had any children and my wife and I lived alone for many years. After my wife died I followed in my father's footsteps, collecting black horses and going from village to village sharpening knives. While trudging through the winters and the springs, one day I met Ferman on Mangal Mountain. I could sense that I was tired. My hands weren't as strong as they used to be when sharpening knives and I often cut my fingers. I needed to stop and rest on the soil where I would be buried. Ferman told me to be an imam in the mosque of this village and promised to look after the horses on the moors himself."

Haco and Kewê took care of each other, like birds who knew the value of the solitary grains left over on the threshing floor. Life was a silently flowing river. The two old people awoke in the mornings together and worked in their small garden together. The sky was here today, gone tomorrow. When they fell ill they breathed their own lives into the fever on their brows, when they couldn't sleep they stared into the darkness together. People were people's best refuge. They sat under the apple tree and told romantic fairy stories to the little girl who was my mother.

My mother also shared Haco and Kewê's happiness. Their breath warmed her on cold nights and she believed their hands were as sublime as elderly trees. My mother sometimes took them for two orphans and she would throw her tiny arms around them and stroke their sweat-soaked hair in their sleep. Every child prepared itself to carry the world on its shoulders; my mother took charge of two worlds at once.

When Haco collapsed to the ground that night, like every good person departing this world his face relaxed, releasing its tension. He took a deep breath. His mother, whom he had last seen when he was three years old, appeared before him. He understood that death was not a bad thing and spoke in strained tones, like the weary turning of an old grinding stone.

"The black horses are coming from far away."

Kewê closed Haco's eyes and pulled the quilt over his face. She took down the Qur'an hanging on the wall and placed it beside his head. A red breeze blew in through the open door. Kewê realized that her life was flowing before her eternally, like a river that can't stop, and that she had lost count of all the deaths she had witnessed. She looked at my mother sitting on the ground in despair and saw before her a little girl experiencing a different form of loneliness in this world. She told her to go to the spring, to wash her face and to fetch water, to keep her away from death's oppression.

My mother went out into the darkness. She raised her head and looked up at the starry sky. She walked slowly in her bare feet. Tonight she saw the soil more as a hungry child than a fertile mother and went to the apple tree and wept silently. She did not startle the birds waiting amongst the branches and quietly tied a rag around a low-hanging branch. She put her head under the cool water of the fountain and sat on a stone carved with ancient Roman scripts until she was sated with crying. She remembered the song that said "You can't appreciate sunshine without rain, nor spring without winter." Without death you couldn't appreciate the preciousness of life. As the poet said:

The joy of loving and sleeping together,
Every lover agrees.

Death is just as enamoured of life.
Death is just as enamoured of life.

Ferman, who had roamed alone for so many years, was like the wind after he adopted Haco's black horses. One moment he was on this side of Haymana Plain, the next at the other end. He traversed every inch of the mountains and discovered the goings on of the nearby villages by chatting to the shepherds. When he came across the valley that was the grizzly bear's hiding spot he became its guardian angel, refusing to allow caravans or shepherds anywhere near it. The soldiers he had occasionally scrapped with were no longer after him, they had left him alone since the declaration of the amnesty.

Ferman thought that time in the village had frozen. Life there had come to a halt sixteen years ago. If he had approached the village he would have seen it was still snowing, just like on that winter night when he had shot his brothers. He believed that, lost his temper with anyone who didn't and pointed his gun at them. He prepared himself to die alone on the moors.

Once someone bowed to their destiny they had nothing to wait for but the moment of their death. Ferman dug himself a grave. He lit a fire by the graveside and sang folk-songs. If losing his mind had any comfort it was that he grew accustomed to his solitude there and lived that way until he met Tatar the photographer. But the gate to the garden of destiny had not yet closed. The day Ferman looked at the photos Tatar gave him his mind became cloudy. A moss-grown stone in his soul suddenly cracked. He held Asya's photograph between his slender fingers like a mirror that might slip and fall, and while he looked at her face he remembered himself. Sometimes a human mind needed a reflection. This was Ferman's first look at such a mirror since he had taken to the moors.

When the Claw-faced woman's twin daughters suddenly appeared Ferman was not startled. He had just woken from a sleep that had lasted for years. He let the girls ride the black horses and took them round the hills. He rolled cigarettes for them as though they were adults. When he asked, "Who are you?" the girls burst out laughing and threw their arms around him. They said they were Asya's confidantes. Ferman, who for years had paid no heed to travellers or to any sensible shepherd, believed the small girls. He took them to his grave and lit a huge bonfire. He said that when he died they were to bury him in that grave. The girls said, "Don't worry, we'll bury you here and dance above your head." Then, tossing their hair from side to side, they danced around the grave with their hands in the air. They were as cheerful as the fairies that appeared before shepherds in the night. Ferman laughed too and danced arm in arm with them until he was exhausted. Completely out of breath and soaked with sweat, he stretched out on the ground and gazed at the shooting stars above his head. The girls talked to him about Asya. They told him that Asya too lay down beside graves at night and dreamed while gazing up at the stars. Then they played a game; one of the girls cried as though she were Asya, while the other roamed around her like a horseman, pretending to be Ferman. Ferman understood that these girls and Asya were all like him.

As the full moon was ascending high in the sky the twin girls said, "Come on, let's go."

"Where to?" asked Ferman.

"Where do you think? To Asya."

At that moment the skies thundered and a ray of lightning struck in the south. They didn't understand what had occurred on that crystal-clear night. As my father was struck by lightning on the opposite hill while guarding sheep, Ferman and the twin girls gazed up in wonder at the infinite sky. Then they mounted the black horses. Leaving the roaring fire to fend for itself, they rode headlong into the darkness.

16
SHE

The Tree of Life

The train pulled slowly out of the station.

As I looked at the girl sitting opposite me I remembered Tolstoy's words, and thought: Happy people are all alike; every unhappy person is unhappy in their own way.

The girl cradled her tea in her hands as though she felt cold and looked at me out of the corner of her eye.

Her unhappiness was hidden on the side of her face that wasn't revealing any secrets. She was one month pregnant and she hadn't told her lover, who was married to someone else.

The girl wasn't drinking tea to stay awake, but to forget her misery.

She had a melancholy kind of beauty.

This was a game I liked playing with myself. I would observe strangers while travelling and invent their life stories.

The day was just beginning to grow light.

I was on my way to Norwich to interpret. A patient at the university hospital was having a kidney transplant and I had to be there in two hours.

The passengers on the early morning train still bore the marks of the previous day. They weren't a hospital worker, a university student, a company manager, but unhappy people all wanting to forget the miserable events of the day before. Besides, happy people were all alike.

It had been three weeks since Feruzeh had gone to Iran. I didn't know if she was coming back or not. Neither did Azita.

Azita returned from London. I went to visit her.

Stella came out of hospital. I went to her antique shop several times to help her out.

I didn't see O'Hara again. The previous day I had bought a loaf of bread from their stall in the market. His father told me the parcel I was expecting should arrive by the following week.

The time was drawing near.

I needed to look for flight tickets and tell Azita I was going to Iran.

There was no news from Feruzeh.

Uncertainty weighed heavier than time.

The life I lived in this small city only a month ago was now as remote as a stone that has fallen over the edge of a precipice.

I broke my own record for the past year when I fainted three times in a week. I wasn't unduly concerned.

Being alone bothered me much more.

At night when I was half asleep I would raise my head and check my phone to see if anyone had called.

I couldn't be sure whether what was happening to me was real or not.

My past was behind a curtain. I had to go to Feruzeh. I had to see her so I could open the curtain of both the future and the past.

The train sped past green fields.

Mist draped the trees and hills in the distance.

I turned my head and caught the eye of the girl sitting opposite.

I wondered what she could see in my face.

What kind of a mirror was I to her?

I lowered my eyes.

I took a book out of my bag and opened it at the page where I had left off the night before. The novel was about the separation of happiness and a mind at peace. People might sometimes have to renounce one for the sake of the other.

I should tell the girl sitting opposite that.

The train stopped at a station.

I raised my head from the book.

The platform was crowded. A young couple, an old woman struggling to carry her bag and a man talking on his mobile phone passed by my window.

I closed my eyes, as though I were going to sleep.

I leaned my head against the window.

I listened to the sound of the tracks as the train slowly pulled away.

Train journeys reminded me of big cities. Old streets, skyscrapers, shadowy love affairs, a yearning for subversion, torture, fancy lifestyles and poverty flashed before my eyes.

The monotonous sound of the tracks soon made me drowsy.

I may have fallen asleep. Sometimes it was difficult to tell daydreams and reality apart.

I raised my head.

I looked out of the window at the green fields, the hills and the villages in the distance.

The girl sitting opposite me had dozed off. Her head was tilted to one side, her pained expression was now relaxed. She didn't seem to be breathing.

She didn't open her eyes until we reached Norwich station.

She smiled at me as we got off the train.

I understood her expression. She had read my face and perceived that I was unhappy.

I slipped away from the crowd.

I hurried to the hospital.

The operation went on until after midday. I paced up and down as anxiously as the patient's relatives until I heard that the operation had been a success. I felt relieved as I translated the doctors' kind, reassuring words.

On the way out I bought a cup of tea from the outdoor café and sat down. I noticed that the girl I had seen on the train earlier was now sitting beside me.

She looked happy. The morning's despondency was wiped off her face and she was humming a song to herself. She was holding a magazine and flicking through the brightly coloured pages.

I took my phone out of my bag.

Whilst checking my messages I knocked over the teacup in front of me. I leapt up to stop the tea from spilling over me and dropped my phone.

As I was picking it up I saw that it was switched on. I breathed a sigh of relief.

One of the messages was from Feruzeh.

It said, "I'm in Cambridge. Phone me."

Feruzeh was back.

I read the message several times.

I looked around me.

I met the eyes of the girl on the train. She was happy and now I was too.

I took a deep breath.

I went outside and leaned against the opposite wall.

I called Feruzeh.

The telephone rang.

"Hello Feruzeh," I said.

"Brani Tawo ..."

Her voice was both distant and very near.

"Welcome back," I said.

"Were you asleep? Are you at home?" she asked.

"No, I'm in Norwich. I've been interpreting," I said.

"So that's why your phone was switched off," she said.

"When did you get back?"

"This morning."

"You should have told me you were coming," I said.

"I couldn't. I'll tell you everything."

"I take it you're here to stay?"

"Yes, I'm here to stay," she said.

"Can we meet today?"

"Yes. What time will you be here?"

"I'm on my way to the train station. I'll be there in two hours," I said.

"Where shall we meet?"

"In the Fort St George. The first place we went to ..."

"Okay," she said.

I didn't check the bus stop. I hailed the taxi that was coming towards me and went to the station.

I ran to the platform.

I just about made the train.

It pulled away the moment I sat down.

I leaned back and caught my breath.

I immersed myself in the sound of the rail tracks.

If everyone makes a journey they will never forget then perhaps this one would be mine.

All the terrible possibilities that had been torturing me for weeks were wiped out of my mind.

I looked out of the window.

The hills and small towns were ablaze in the late afternoon sunshine.

Horses plodded in the pastures flanking the green fields.

I was gazing out at life like a child on its first visit to a city.

I was the last one on the train and the first one off at Cambridge.

As I strode away I heard Feruzeh's voice.

"Brani Tawo …"

I looked around me.

Feruzeh was waving to me from the other end of the platform.

I walked through the buzz of the crowd.

"Welcome back," she said.

"No, you welcome back," I said.

I hugged her silently.

Then I looked at her face.

She was thinner. She had dark rings under her eyes.

"You've lost weight," I said.

She smiled.

"It's very crowded here."

"What made you come to the station? We were supposed to meet at the pub," I said.

"There's an empty bench here, let's sit down a moment," she said.

We wove through the crowd and sat down on the bench a little further ahead.

It was cool.

The sun had gone down behind the roofs.

I thought Feruzeh must be cold so I took my cardigan out of my bag and put it around her shoulders.

Feruzeh, who had refused my jacket by the church on the night we first met now responded with a smile.

"Is everything all right in Iran?" I said.

"It seems to be."

"How's Roya?"

"She's better, she's back on her feet," she said.

"That's good news," I said.

Feruzeh hesitated.

"Did you know she tried to commit suicide?" she said.

"I guessed. How is her relationship with her husband?"

"Fine."

Feruzeh started sniffing.

I took a tissue out of my bag and gave it to her.

"Are you all right?" I said.

"Fine," she said. "The bridge between Roya and me was broken; we needed to repair it."

"If this hadn't suddenly happened you might never have made up," I said.

"I realize that she lives in two worlds, one with me in it and one with her husband."

"Iran's in one, Britain's in the other ..." I said.

Feruzeh stopped and looked at me.

"Roya tried to die because she wanted to have a firmer hold on life," she said.

"I hope that from now on she'll hold on to life as tightly as you do," I said.

She paused for a moment and then took a deep breath.

"It's the first time I've been back to Iran since I was a child," she said.

"How did you feel?"

"Shall I tell you how I felt? I wanted to grow a tree here that would be the same as a tree in Tehran, just like your grandmother Kewê's apple tree."

"You should," I said.

"I didn't get a chance this time. But next time I'm going to choose myself an apple tree and bring the seeds back to plant here," she said.

A train pulled in to the station.

The waiting passengers moved towards the platform.

"How are you? What have you been up to?" asked Feruzeh.

"The usual stuff. The only thing that's changed is that now I see more of Stella."

"I went to see her too. I dropped by the antique shop before I came here," she said.

I laughed. "She's even more cheerful in that shop now than she was before," I said.

"Stella showed me something," she said.

"What?"

"Guess."

"Has my camera arrived?"

"A friend of Stella's brought it from London this morning."

"Really? It must be my day today," I said.

"It's a sharp, sound machine," she said.

"An Olympus Six, isn't it?"

"Yes."

"At last," I said. "If I ever go home I won't go to my mother empty-handed."

"You told Stella the story about the camera."

"I was going to tell you first but I never got the chance," I said.

"Shall we both go and see Stella tomorrow?" she said.

"Yes, let's."

"Then you and I can have a little chat," she said.

"What about?" I said.

Feruzeh swallowed.

"Sins ..." she said.

"I couldn't fit all my sins into just tomorrow," I said.

She looked at me with a sad, weary expression.

"I'm being serious," she said.

"So am I," I said.

The buzz in the station got louder.

Feruzeh started coughing.

I passed her the bottle of water from my bag.

"You seem to have everything in that bag," she said.

I opened the bag and looked inside.

"I've given you everything that was inside, the only thing left is a book," I said.

"Which book?"

"A novel."

I took it out.

"Is it in Turkish?" she asked.

"Yes," I replied.

"What's it called?"

"*A Mind at Peace.*"

"Is it good?"

"That doesn't matter," I said.

Feruzeh stopped. She waited for the buzzing on the platform to stop.

"Why are you reading it then?" she said.

"Do you know what the difference is between how I felt before you left and how I feel now?" I said.

"What?"

"The answer is in this book. Do you want to find out what it is?"

"I most certainly do," she said.

I passed her the book.

"Open any page," I said.

Feruzeh opened a page. She scrutinized the words, as though they would mean something to her, then she passed it to me.

"There's a folk-song here for you," I said.

Feruzeh looked at me.

"Would I have got the same folk-song no matter which page I opened?" she said.

"Yes," I said. "It's not just your family that plays this kind of game."

She laughed.

"What sort of folk-song?"

"When I was telling you about my grandmother Kewê's life I mentioned a folk-song she sang, do you remember?"

"The folk-song she heard in the fields one night, and that she then sang to your mother, isn't that the one?"

"You haven't forgotten," I said.

"Why would I forget …?"

"You wanted to hear the song that day, but I didn't sing it to you. All in good time they say. I had a very hard time while you were away and now the time has come for that song."

Feruzeh picked up the bag separating us, put it on the ground and moved closer to me.

"I told you I had never sung that song to anyone before," I said.

"Yes."

She looked into my eyes.

"After the song will you tell me a story too? I've missed your stories," she said.

"Do you want a radio story?"

"Yes Brani Tawo," she said. "Tell me one of the stories you used to listen to on the radio when you were a little boy."

"Okay," I said.

Feruzeh's knee touched my knee, and her breath touched my breath.

She waited in silence.

I closed my eyes and started singing the song. I tilted my head to the side, just as Kewê used to do when she was singing it to my mother and my mother used to do when she was singing it to me.

A red breeze blew. The branches rustled.

Then time stood still.

Brani Tawo: "I have always hesitated to put the feelings in my heart into words Feruzeh."

Feruzeh: "Why?"

Brani Tawo: "I was afraid of us both getting hurt."

Feruzeh: "Why would we get hurt?"

Brani Tawo: "Perhaps my fears were unfounded, I don't know."

The hum of the station crowd. The rumble of a train.

Feruzeh: "Brani Tawo, when I was telling your poetry fortune in my book of secrets I saw our shared future."

Brani Tawo: "You didn't tell me that."

Feruzeh: "I was going to tell you when the time was right."

Brani Tawo: "There's a novel I read many years ago, I feel as though I'm a character in that novel."

Feruzeh: "What kind of a novel?"

Brani Tawo: "A man is in love with a woman but he can't tell her of his feelings."

Feruzeh: "Does he never put his feelings into words?"

Brani Tawo: "One day the man plucks up the courage and tells the woman what his mind fears but his heart desires."

Feruzeh: "What does the woman do?"

Brani Tawo: "That doesn't matter, what matters is the end."

The noise in the station grows louder. A train whistles.

Feruzeh: "What happens at the end of the novel?"

Brani Tawo: "The woman commits suicide."

Feruzeh: "That means she loves him."

Brani Tawo: "If everyone who loves dies I want to spare you that fate, Feruzeh."

Feruzeh: "And the only way of doing that is by remaining silent?"

Brani Tawo: "What my mind fears but my heart desires is ..."
Feruzeh: "Be quiet and kiss me."

Silence.

Feruzeh: "I've waited so long for this moment. Kiss me again."

Silence.
The silence continues.
The rumble of a train grows more and more distant.

The End

GLOSSARY

Agha: an identifying title signifying status. Literally lord.

Bayram: religious festival, holiday or feast day.

Börek: a sweet or savoury pastry typically but not exclusively made with meat or cheese, and which can be baked, griddled or fried.

Deniz (Gezmiş): a Turkish socialist revolutionary and political activist. He was executed in 1972, aged twenty-five, by a military tribunal for "attempting to overthrow constitutional order". Today he is a national hero in left-wing circles. (The word Deniz means "sea" in Turkish.)

Gecekondu: literally "sprung up overnight". A cheap, illegal dwelling constructed very quickly by people migrating from rural areas to the outskirts of large cities.

Hut: an ogre-like giant in Kurdish folk-tales.

Leyla and Mecnun: a classic Arab story based on the story of a real man called Mecnun who fell in love with Leyla and went mad when her father prevented him from marrying her. The word *mecnun* means "madman".

Burhan Sönmez

Lokum: traditional Turkish confectionery known as Turkish delight, often flavoured with almonds, pistachios, rosewater or lemon.

Mukhtar: the head of a village or neighbourhood.

Zamzam water: according to Muslims, miraculously generated water from the well of Zamzam in Mecca. It is visited by millions of pilgrims each year, who drink its water for its healing properties.

TRANSLATOR'S BIOGRAPHY

Ümit Hussein is a British translator and interpreter of Turkish Cypriot origin. She was born and raised in London. She made her debut in the world of translation and interpretation at the age of five, when she would accompany her mother and grandmother to the consulting rooms of medical, legal and other professionals as their interpreter. Having acquired a taste for words and languages, she studied Italian and European Literature before going on to get an MA in Literary Translation from the University of East Anglia. During the course of her career she has translated well-known names such as Nevin Halıcı, Mehmet Yashin and Ahmet Altan into English. Today she lives between Seville and London and combines her literary pursuits with interpreting.